The Con

JD DeLuzio

Milton, Ontario
http://www.brain-lag.com/

Brain Lag Publishing
Ontario, Canada
http://www.brain-lag.com/

Cover artwork by Catherine Fitzsimmons

Library and Archives Canada Cataloguing in Publication

Title: The con / J.D. DeLuzio.
Names: DeLuzio, Jeff, author.
Identifiers: Canadiana (print) 20200316052 | Canadiana (ebook) 20200316168 | ISBN 9781928011415
   (softcover) | ISBN 9781928011422 (EPUB)
Classification: LCC PS8557.E463 C66 2020 | DDC C813/.54—dc23

The Con and Related Stories

The Con..7

Troll Bridge...183

Do You See What I See?.....................................215

To years of lives

The Con

"One half of the world cannot understand the
pleasures of the other."
—Jane Austen, *Emma*

1
Stop Me If You've Heard This One

So this fat old nerd, two genius fangirls, a Klingon and his brother, and Lady Susan Vernon get on an elevator. The Klingon and his brother both glance at the older woman, but their hopes and eyes rest on the female fen—vivacious, pretty Chelsea, in particular. It is a truth universally acknowledged that an SF fan in possession of a Klingon outfit must be in need of a girlfriend.

Elsewhere, the athlete makes her way to the hotel, and Miss Moon settles into her room.

Patti Washington greets me, and her friend Chelsea brims over with recognition. Patti is the obvious genius; we all know that, but I've learned not to underestimate Chelsea. Beneath the bubble of babbling Barbie, she can at least keep pace with her friend. They've been coming to this con since they were fanbrats of fourteen. They must be ready to graduate high school, assuming Patti hasn't fast-tracked her way through the tedium of formal education and started her PhD. I recall her that first year, sitting and talking to a science panel headed by Vernor Vinge, like the boy Jesus at the temple.

Thomas, the older brother, eyes Chelsea, and he's about to speak when Mark, through his gruff alien exterior, squeaks out, "*wanI'.tIv!*"

Patti arches an eyebrow. "Do you want to buy a vowel?" she asks.

So Mark actually *speaks* Klingon. He looks strangely uncomfortable in the make-up, the latex ridges on his forehead and the costume, a bit of space armour over basic black and, even here, he's anomalous if anything can be. *Star Trek*'s Klingons as costume are in a lull just now. Most cosplayers run either with the trendy or the terribly obscure. Some make obscurity a virtue, in fact, with recognition constituting a secret handshake. Maybe Mark just wants to be a warrior. I don't think he's been much of a warrior in his short life.

"I was, I mean..." He stumbles, awkwardly, for words. "That's good. See, I was trying to welcome you to the con, but I don't know a Klingon word for *con*. Um. So I went with *wanI'*... Yeah."

The elevator stops on seventh. Chelsea's smile is not unfriendly. Patti says, "It's a big universe. I'm sure there's a planet where what you said makes perfect sense."

"We'll see you boys around the *wanI'*," says Chelsea. She precedes Patti out the door, raising her arms against the incoming crowd, clearing the way for her friend through a baffled family of Mundanes and a smallish creature in a hood, a sort of walking fish with salmon skin and well-crafted cat eyes. Patti walks confidently but, with her twisted hobble, awkwardly. The Mundanes and the fish-creature enter the elevator. The fish tickles something in the back of my brain, but I cannot recall from whose story it comes.

"Nice one," says Thomas, smugly, to his embarrassed alien brother.

"I thought *I'd* stand out," says Lady Susan, eyeing the hooded fish. The Mundane parents have that cornered look, but their young daughter seems amused.

The light dawns and I ask, "Are the Austenites meeting at this hotel?"

"Janeites." Lady Susan nods. "But we're not nearly so many as your group."

"So, are you Lady Susan Vernon?"

She curtsies. "Very good."

"You'll have a lot of company in costume this weekend." I've had my share of failure around women but, next to the brothers, I'm smooth as a Peak District lake. I glance again at the fish-creature. It has nostril slits near the top of its face; I suspect that's how the wearer actually sees out—or rather, one wearer, for its four legs suggested two smallish people had crammed into the outfit. Judging from the placement of the arms, they must belong to the cosplayer at the back. A marvel of costume engineering, and damned familiar. It came from no movie, I'm now certain, but when I file through SF novels and short stories I cannot find a match. Am I experiencing extraterrestrial aphasia? I shiver, just a little, and much will transpire before I remember. *Best Original* always produces the most fascinating costumes at the masquerade. I expect this one will take best in show, up against various Avengers and cumoms, and video game characters that I won't recognize.

"You know, she's one of Miss Austen's most consistently underrated characters," says Lady Susan. "However did you identify me?"

"Don't sound so surprised," I say. She's beginning to sound like someone else I know, and the coincidence of *her* gathering being crammed into the hotel space left unoccupied by the SF con feels like a plot device from a Regency novel.

She reads my con badge. "Telfryn. That is a most interesting name."

"Telfryn Tyde," I say, extending a hand, and wonder if that violates Regency etiquette. We wish each other well, and she exits onto the eighth floor.

Mark the Klingon came looking for love. *Nga'chuq.* So did his brother. He started on his makeup hours ago, while I sat in a church basement with Denise

Moon. He has a plan. He hopes that, as he circulates Friday, he might, from behind the safety of his mask, draw the curious, and perhaps gain the attention of some hot fen in ears or anime outfits. Then he would make the Saturday evening party rounds as himself, reconnect with some of those same girls, maybe one special girl.

Some of what I relate I learned from a drunken and lovesick Mark a con later. I used sources where I could. The remaining absent spaces I've filled through otherworldly guidance. I like to believe I'm close enough to the truth.

This is the Gospel according to Telfryn.

2
Saving the World with Denise Moon

I should say that what I'd been doing with Denise Moon earlier that day was sorting canned and packaged food. The other food drives never achieve the heights of activity and can-stacks we see at midwinter, but they try. Now as then, the food bank maintains a flurry of activity while looking scandalously empty, because all of the regular volunteers are out picking up donations and we're understaffed at HQ. After the tragic turn in my twenties, I learned what it was like to rely on the kindness of people I would never meet. So I'm usually the volunteer left running the show while the schools and churches bring us beans and Kraft Dinner and things discovered at the backs of shelves. Denise is a regular volunteer whose church pulls off miraculous hauls of donations. They needed help organizing at end-of-summer, and that was enough to get me into their rectory basement.

I immediately recognized the boyish-faced minister. I lurk in libraries and peruse places that sell second-hand books, and I attended their summer rummage sale with Brian Slesak. We cleaned them out of the few solid SF paperbacks they had that we hadn't yet read. It happened the book table had a cardboard box labelled *Discount Theological Books*. I remarked to Brian that the box gave good advice and Brian laughed his full braying laugh. The pastor, lingering behind me, retained his shiny appearance and polished personality—he even managed a smile—but the old ladies working the place looked scandalized, and I could tell in that instant that the pastor cared very much for the feelings of the old ladies. Such a creature oversaw the sorting that morning. The Old Lady and the Pastor worked closer to the little stage on one end of the basement; Denise and I sorted foodstuff on the main floor.

Belief in God be damned—they're feeding the hungry.

Did Miss Moon pull me in? I have no delusions about myself. Even if I were a decade younger and Korean, she wouldn't be interested. I drew attention from women once but, by the time I understood that I did, Augusta had married Brian, and I had fallen deep into my crack-up. The loss of sanity and gainful employment left me focused on other matters. I make money now, to be sure, but my job as a clerk hardly nets what I made during those brief, shining years in chemical waste management. Time travel, alas, is not an option. I say this to Denise, after giving her an abridged and bowdlerized account of my life.

"But wouldn't you like to see the past?" Denise Moon puts three more boxes of macaroni and cheese in their appointed places. "I'm a huge reader of historical fiction," she says. "And"—here she lowers her eyes a moment—"I belong to the Jane Austen Society. I'd love to go to a Regency Ball."

"You'd stand out at a Regency Ball."

"Well. It's not as though it would happen."

When I think of time travel, I think about my own life. But if I could do things over, what, then? Could I have prevented the breakdown of my own chemical nature, if I knew in advance it was going to occur? If I'd recognized Augusta's feelings, would we have been happy? Would she have nursed me back to health, ensured the medicinal regiment that keeps me sane, or would I have simply laid low a woman who now seems perfectly content married to Brian, their daughters models of responsibility and normalcy? Would I, if I could go back, not be plagued with the desire to prevent crimes, disasters of which I would have foreknowledge? And if I placed a call, say, warning of the 9-11 terrorist attacks or some notorious killing, would it be traced, and would I be rotting in a prison across the border?

Could I have saved Stumbo, or would I have just driven him further into his dark paranoia?

At lunch, I ask Miss Moon about the Jane Austen Society, a group I have hitherto lumped with Yaohnanen cargo cultists and furries. We sit on the floor surrounded by piles of processed food and hygiene products, like children in a schoolyard amidst playground equipment. The Pastor and the Old Lady eat in the kitchen.

"In Toronto," she says. "It's a small meeting of people from different chapters... Most of the local group are older women... Our chapter president's husband, of course, who is a retired English teacher. A few are a bit younger. I'm our group secretary, so of course they really wanted me to be there."

Toronto, I reflect, but I suppose that mentioning I would be heading in that general direction might reveal too much. I find her muted enthusiasm oddly engaging. I know her group also cosplays, Regency-era ball-gowns and great coats, Beau Brummel cravats.

"Well, there's usually a reading or a musical performance at our larger gatherings. The performers might wear some sort of costume. And there's one very interesting woman, about my age—we're rooming together—who always arrives as a character. Apparently she's doing Lady Susan Vernon this year."

"I don't know that character," I say. "But I don't know Jane Austen."

"Oh. It's okay. Most people are not acquainted with Lady Susan. She's from an early book of Jane's that wasn't published during her life. A rather unusual book for its time; Lady Susan is a wicked woman, a conniver out for a wealthy husband, but she receives less consequences than you'd expect, for a book of that era… Sorry, you probably find this tremendously dull."

"No. I'm fascinated by the trivialities that people, that become so important…" I'm uncertain how to finish the sentence, because her smile fades.

"Well, we should return to real work then," she says. I want to tell her that I meant *triviality* in a literal and non-pejorative sense, that I often immerse myself in trivialities, but I assume that anything I say now will be taken with some other shading. We pass the rest of the afternoon more silently than the morning, and with fewer pleasantries. We part with cool amicability, which the pastor and his assistants—for he acquired a second and a third Old Lady in the afternoon—might have even noticed. He approaches me just before I leave.

"Thank you for your help, and God bless you."

"Anytime I can help with anything practical."

"Yes. Of course. I know you didn't ask me, Telfryn, but I think a man is wise to ask questions. Still, I wouldn't *discount* the role of God."

"Of course," I say, a little surprised. Awaiting a denouement like, *God has not discounted you*, I smile. What else can I do? We shake hands and part. He's pleasant and sincere, and I can't dislike him.

I catch my ride out front of the church. Augusta and Brian Slesak unfailingly drive me to any con they are also attending, and they've been attending more now that their girls are older.

3
The Odyssey

As I step off the curb and throw my luggage into the popped trunk, Mark and Thomas are crossing the Bluewater Bridge in their battered premillennial Honda Odyssey, with fuzzy icosahedral dice hanging from the rear view. Mark has his shoulder armor and make-up readily available, so he can start his final transformation to Klingon once they arrive in Canada.

"We need a sign to put on the door," says Thomas, as they idle in line, and he ensures his passport is handy. He thinks back to residence life last year, and of a cute but clingy engineering student named Jasmine.

"A sign?" asks Mark.

"If one of us has some hot fangirl in our room..." He thinks a minute, while his brother whistles a bar of the *Sailor Moon* theme. "Do we still have all those purple twist ties in the glove compartment?"

"Yeah, we haven't figured out a use for them yet."

The line moves forward, one more car. "Okay. Okay. We'll take them into the room. If you see a purple twist tie around the doorknob, you go back to the game room and slay a few more orcs."

"Why not just text?"

"Mark, Mark. You can't always discreetly text, and girls will take offense if they're getting all hot and you whip out your cell phone. Also, you really don't wanna break the pacing. Whereas you have a reason to check the door, ensure that it's locked. 'Cause then you're just thinking of them."

"What if we... What if we both get lucky?" Mark asks.

"Then I'll sell Satan a snowspeeder."

Mark lets it pass. He knows it's the truth. Big brother is driving him. That's enough.

They reach the Canadian highway. It's an easy pass, minus time spent explaining what a "con" is to the curious official in the booth.

As Thomas and Mark head down the 402, Patti and Chelsea are boarding the bus from their Lake Huron hometown. Kate the Athlete, having made her plan and confirmed with Aunt Izzy, struggles to arrange transportation—a parental lift to nearby Stratford, Ontario, and then the train. The Janeites, the ones already in Toronto, no doubt finish High Tea—loose-leaf, with visions of the weekend's syllabus and syllabub dancing in their heads. By late afternoon I'm looking out the window at the airport strip, the future imagined decades earlier, elevated freeways and buildings and concrete everywhere. Augusta and Brian have a room one floor up, at her insistence far from the elevator. I hold no such reservations; I've learned to live with background sounds and voices in the night.

4

Stranger in a Strange Land

Flights below, Kate the Athlete enters the hotel lobby. A pretty teen girl painted green passes by; Kate inhales deeply. Two of Doctor Who's incarnations kick back and chat. One of them checks her out. A polyester lizard makes for the lounge. Not a few of the con-badged are heavier and unhealthier than Kate cares to see. If the *fen* are as smart as Chelsea claims, why don't they take better care of their bodies?

She has two texts, one from Aunt Izzy, responding to the news of her safe arrival. One more is from her mother. She expects the next might be further shade from Steve and Lucas about the Challenge. But she's heard nothing more from Chelsea since Chelsea texted that she and Patti had safely arrived and she'd see her on Monday, and tell her all about the con.

A man runs into the lobby, laughing maniacally. He spreads open his long trenchcoat to reveal a superhero outfit: the Flash. People chuckle appreciatively. A few give raucous cheer. Kate does a slow blink of blue eyes and finally exhales.

It's been a rough ride, for a girl whose life has been regimented and organized, with forms and documentation, since she was a tyke. For all of her toughness—she battled with the boys on the streets and playgrounds, and terrifies her girlier opponents—Kate's parents and coaches have overseen her, every step of the way. And she doesn't consider herself rebellious. But now she's two hundred kilometres from home under false pretenses, on the outskirts of the Megacity, at an airport strip hotel commandeered by nerds. Worse—she will miss the Rose Point Challenge for the first time since she was invited to play (excepting tournaments and finals. You get a pass for *real* sporting events). It's just a pickup game, played late afternoon one Sunday each month, but it is by invitation only, and she's the lone female to have received the tap in the Challenge's illustrious history. Lucas and Steve most pushed for her nomination. They blow it off—lots of people miss in summer, family vacations and job hours—but she knows they're baffled.

A bespeckled woman sits at the registration desk, wearing a tee-shirt with a message that Kate isn't even going to try to decipher, layers of insular meaning, a reference made in a movie she's never watched to a book she's never read concerning a sedentary game she'll never play. A weekend pass runs twenty for a teen. She takes her badge and a program and looks for a place to think through her next manoeuvre. She has a quotation on her bedroom wall: *She who fails to plan, plans to fail.* She's been flailing in improvised play all day. Convincing her parents to let her visit Uncle Phil and Aunt Izzy so she could check out U of Toronto—that worked. Izzy and Phil have been inviting her up all year. She's about to hit eleventh grade, but she already has a scholarship offer from a minor Midwestern college in the U.S. But U of T? That's closer to home, and carries prestige.

Aunt Izzy knows more about Kate's actual reasons, because Izzy figured out Kate by the time her niece hit thirteen.

Planning got her to the Greater Toronto Area with few suspicions. She has no idea how Phase Two is supposed to work. She's still not ready to e-connect, which is what anyone sane would have already done. She wants to surprise Chels. But real-world stalking? How did *that* become an option? She looks up from the bench in the lobby. A skinny bespectacled blond guy in a red shirt walks by. He turns his head to check her out and strolls casually into a Regency soldier. She returns to her planning. Chelsea's somewhere in this madness, and she needs to be prepared for when she finds her.

5
My God, It's Full of Starfruit!

Chelsea, at that moment, could be found sitting in a room reserved in Patti's father's name, reflecting on things that haven't happened. She recalls months of Katie, getting closer to Katie, mismatched classroom friends, sideways glances over the planning of D-Day and the conductivity of pure substances. And the jocks asking Kate, "does she ever talk about...? I mean, it was *them*, right?"

At the start of the previous school year she and Patti hacked the Board of Education. Patti figured Tech Club needed a reputation makeover. She assured Chelsea she didn't care about popularity. But notoriety? A shot across the bow and don't anyone be fucking with us or ours! They tweaked a laptop and jacked the Wi-Fi from the local hotel. Suddenly, people clicking anywhere on the Board of Education site—days before Grade Nine Parents Night—got redirected to an online video of "You Are a Pirate!"

from that Icelandic kids' show. A cheap ploy, to be sure, because Pirates have been the school's team since '35—the school's mascot, a parrot in a tricorne, often seen swinging a toy sword on the sidelines. Law enforcement couldn't trace the hack further than the Wi-Fi in the local hotel, couldn't prove a thing, which meant everyone knew it had to be Patti and Chelsea. Sitting in the office, recognizing that neither school admin nor cops knew anything, Patti helpfully suggested that if someone could so easily hack the board's servers, they needed to tighten security. Just a suggestion, brown eyes blinking. Are we done here yet?

The inhabitants of Teen World threw appreciative nods, began stepping aside faster, polite and a little bit frightened. Patti Washington, Evil Genius. It's a mixed blessing, really, because Chelsea likes these other kids. Chelsea and Kate by then talked together, outside of class, sometimes, picking up where they almost started in grade nine. Chelsea began watching girls' basketball games. Running the scoreboard, even, sometimes.

So by spring Kate can mention a party, the kind Chelsea and Patti roll eyes about: hormonally-turned-up, loud. The partiers eyed them, mismatched friends with matching brunette ponytails, but Chelsea's affable and Kate's a star and a small town lagging a decade behind social attitudes hasn't asked the question aloud yet. And neither has Kate, exactly. The pair left when beer starting spilling from bottles and high-fructose alcohol from red cups, because that isn't Kate's thing either.

Kate walked her home. They talked, eyes wide but a safe space between them. The hug goodnight lasts longer than Regulation Girl.

Chelsea and Patti were sitting in the school library a week later when Lucas and Steve approached them. Lucas is a blond Kal-El minus the spitcurl and alien heritage: farmboy, quarterback, point guard, small-town celebrity. Also math whiz. Patti outthinks him, but he can follow her when she does. Lucas knew he was staring the answer in the face, and couldn't see it. Steve took the time to joke with Chelsea, because after the party they're apparently old friends. But Chelsea keeps an eye on Patti to catch the flash in her eyes:

Given five points on a sphere, show that there is a closed hemisphere that contains at least four of them. Lucas barely had time to blink before Patti said: "Two points on a sphere determine the boundary of a hemisphere. A great circle. If the northern hemisphere doesn't have another two points, then the southern hemisphere has to have two points."

"Of course," Lucas said.

"Well, duh," said Steve.

"Dude, you didn't understand that at all."

"I stop listening when girls talk about great cycles."

Chelsea giggled. "Circles."

"I'll hit him if you want," Lucas offered.

"Perhaps later," Patti said.

"I'll hit myself. That was a fail."

Chelsea patted him on the shoulder.

Kate passed by about then and joined them tableside. Patti saw some of the other library regulars looking over like they were in a club and her table was where the band took their break. Lately, it seemed, their star was rising, though Patti maintained she didn't care, one way or the other. Of all the guys, Kate seems closest to these two. She treats Steve like a brother, bro-hugged him on arrival, in fact, and Patti's sure Lucas has Kate and Chelsea figured out, even if Kate hasn't, but he would never say anything if he did. Kate fist-bumped him and then hugged Chelsea, but all girly and friendly. Chelsea left the library with her. "So I'll see you after school," she said, to Patti. Patti saw Lucas and Steve's eyes follow asses out.

"Anyway," she said.

"Thanks."

"You would have got it."

"You just saw it. Jesus. All we have to do is show the work."

"Like a free throw," Steve said.

It's a pity, she thought. Lucas is Lucas, and she accepted that, untouchable like some kind of copyright character. Redhead Sara had him, a superficially pleasant girl and, predictably, a cheerleader—the kind, Sara is quick to note, who do *real* gymnastics. But Patti felt something else about Steve, despite his intellectual limitations. She wished she didn't. She let herself laugh and Steve looked satisfied. Guys are easy, at least at this level.

She sits on her hotel bed, leafing through the program, her brown eyes behind Buddy Holly specs. The room's theirs, entirely, courtesy of the Professor, who will not be joining them this year. Chelsea pulls on a pink and purple top, and glances in the mirror. "You could have been nicer to the Klingon."

"I always could have been nicer," Patti says. "We ready?" Chelsea puts purple-lensed glasses over doll-sized eyes and throws thumbs up. The girls head to the consuite.

It's a high-calibre consuite, under the direction of a psittacine-haired person named Paulie. Beyond the expected chips and nuts and Peeps, they've got chili and fruit salad and caffeinated bacon. Coffee in three varieties: decaffeinated, regular, and one brewed with caffeinated water. Cans of beer and alcoholized energy drinks will materialize in the bathtub, sometime after eight. For now, it holds ice and soft drinks and water. A prudent Paulie has duct-taped the toilet shut. Patti grabs a PC cola and a strawberry soy milk and scopes out seats near the middle-aged man from the elevator, because she and I have spoken at cons past. Chelsea scoops fruit onto a pair of paper plates and joins her friend. "There's berries and pineapple and starfruit," she says.

"What's up with starfruit?" Patti, considering the green offerings. "It doesn't taste like anything."

"It's shaped like stars."

"So that's all it brings to the table? It's *star-shaped*?"

"Pretty much."

"It's like the boy band of fruit."

"It probably has, like, nutrients."

"That's good," someone says. "Boy band of fruit."

I laugh. We look up to see Mark the Klingon and his brother Thomas.

6
The Augur of Quaoar

My God, it's full of starfruit, I think, recalling *A Space Odyssey* and its tale of a human reborn and reconfigured by alien contact, extra-terrestrial gods perceived as shards of light and past civilizations. Atmospheric, ambient voices express meaning just beyond our understanding. I know I have heard voices of that kind. I recognized them when I first watched that film, back in my teenage years, on a rented VHS. Thinking of *Space Odyssey* I come nearer to recalling the name of the extraterrestrial visitor in the elevator. Hours after the consuite and under darkness and a gold-checked duvet, my brain will know:

Azogo. Uirtkauwea'ki. And a word I cannot attempt to say, which my brain translates as *Augur*.

I've already described Azogo itself, a squat fish without fins. Its race, the Uirtkauwea, ranges in colour, from Azogo's salmon-rose to gold-yellow and aquamarine blue. They have soulful eyes recalling those of a Terran cat. They're hexapedal, walking on the posterior and anterior limbs and using the longer, central two (which each have three multi-jointed fingers) as we would arms and hands. Reproductively, they most resemble Terran gastropods, and any mature member of the species can impregnate any other.

When they wear clothes—for their culture lacks entirely our sense of physical modesty—it consists of a hooded robe, sometimes with extended sleeves for their limbs. Feet and hands and face they cover only when environmental conditions require it. They can, in fact, endure greater extremes of temperature than most humans, and, due to their planet's larger size and consequentially stronger gravity, they possess greater natural strength.

Like us, the Uirtkauwea feel shut up in the infinite expanse of the universe. Their technology, however, permits at present greater opportunities for exploration than ours does. Their most impressive device for probing the vast dimensions of space is the Augur. Over the last two centuries several such devices have stationed themselves on the outer fringes of a dozen nearby solar systems.

The Augur I know sits among some disjointed and scattered rocks on the bleak surface of Quaoar. Its artificial brain has been fashioned in the image and likeness of Azogo, a naturalist from *Uirtkauwea'ki*. It went live on May 17, 1980.

7

Telfryn Joncourt Tyde: Secret Origins I

When I was eight I broke a vase while playing alone with my *Empire Strikes Back* figures. It was my mother's favourite vase, and after rocking on the floor and then examining the shattered pieces I left, afraid of what my punishment might be. I took the bus, alone, because kids did that back then, and stepped off near the woods behind Lambton College. I heard something in the trees, a voice not quite human, like an imaginary friend or a hidden predator. *Azogo*, it said. I didn't have money for food and the sky was growing darker and I finally realized I'd have to walk back. A cop found me on the sidewalk in some distress, and took me home and that was it, no Children's Aid or Home Services. My parents had been asking around the neighbourhood and were relieved and confused, but I supposed it had worked because I didn't get punished for the vase—not at the time.

My father got me to help him piece it back together with resin epoxy, a slow process that represented more together-time than we'd had in the previous year. It actually looked fine, if you kept the most damaged side to the wall. A year later I returned home while my mother cleaned the living room. She had moved the furniture to dust and vacuum behind it, and the lamps and the vase she had gathered in the center of the room. I greeted her. She turned, like a creature in a Saturday afternoon horror flick, her face distorted to movie monster with rage.

She sprang on me, striking and slapping without explanation. Afterwards I sat in my room, and held myself and rocked. I gave away my *Empire* figures that week. I was starting to read serious SF by then, and the written stuff proved more intriguing than the shimmering fantasies onscreen.

Neither of us mentioned the incident again.

A decade later I returned to Lambton College.

The internet had just started to creep into society, and I spent much of my time there. It led me to a campus gaming group. The beer went down better while slaying monsters, and store purchase costs less than pub brew. Brian Slesak DMed the group. Then a brainy guy in a trilby hat, he brought with him a high school friend named Kirt, who carried the weight of frustrated anger at the world, but could be witty, occasionally shocking, and quite adept at solving Brian's puzzling traps. Both studied computers. Their classmate Augusta became a regular early on, bringing with her Sonia, a foods major who looked and dressed like a chunky Spice Girl and was probably the first person I knew who read manga.

Augusta played ringette and had run with her high school's track and cross country teams. Like Brian, she had a background in band and a penchant for computers. She also proved a voracious reader of SF, and kept a small collection of *Wonder Woman* comics. Kirt initially questioned her on SF and comic-book matters most trivial, with a general air of incredulity. Alas, poor Kirt was out of his depth with her. He'd had too little experience with female nerds. When the women later proved willing to cook so long as we paid and cleaned, he finally accepted them both. Augusta disliked our unhealthy fare, chips and nuts and turkey pepperoni bits, which we prized as dog treats for people. And Sonia needed guinea pigs for her culinary experiments—she now chefs an upscale west coast establishment.

Augusta had, then as now, a preference for sweats and t-shirts, and dark hair that smelled of floral things. Taller than the rest of us, she inevitably played some kickass Elven-type with a sword. Sonia watched pop-SF but she *read* fantasy, and preferred to wield magic.

"Do you have a girlfriend, Telfryn?" Sonia asked me. We met by chance in the north building caf. She wore a short skirt and thigh-socks and talked about a field trip to a soup plant. "Chickens go in one end," she said, "and cubes come out the other. I mean, basically. Killing, plucking, boning, cooking, cubing. The future is now."

"Soylent Green is chicken!" I said.

"Damn them all to hell," she replied.

"From my cold, dead hands?"

She poked about her plate with a plastic fork. "Seriously, they could make this food so much better." Then she asked about my relationship status. I shrugged, but I could feel the ticking of a beating heart. "Do you know much about Augusta?"

I didn't know what to respond; I considered her something next to angelic, but I couldn't say that to Sonia. "We have our next meeting at your apartment, right?"

"Yepper."

I hugged her goodbye. She had inquired about my relationship status, she who was asked out regularly by guys around campus. I felt light-headed. I did a double take as I went upstairs, seeing for a moment an outsized pair of smiling eyes. It turned out to be a girl in a faded *Cats* tee-shirt.

Two days later when I asked Sonia if she wanted to do a movie, she declined. As a group, sure, she really liked me and all, but not if I thought it would be anything else. I accepted her response with resignation. She seemed neither hot nor cold at our next gaming group. They served mushrooms stuffed with some form of seafood. I slew a Rust Monster.

About a month later I received a call at home, the first of my mysterious calls. A voice sang about wanting me and someone jammed on a flute. I hung up. I reflected on the indistinct female voice: *I want your body! I want your babies!* I recalled the musical bit, conventional jazz on a flute. Had I imagined it?

The second time, Kirt was at my place, and he wondered, as he gnawed on leftover Chinese take-out, if someone had targeted me, for some bizarre reason. I nodded, but excused it as a random thing. He wiped neon-red sauce off his face. Anyway, what woman would be so blatant to call and sing about wanting me, but too shy to simply ask about, say, going for coffee? It made no sense. I asked my mother, who rarely left the house anymore, if she had received any strange calls. She said someone had phoned the night before but hung up when she answered. Then she looked alarmed and I thought it better to say nothing more, to assure her it was probably just a wrong number.

"Well, if you're certain," she said. Her lip trembled, just a bit.

After Kirt left, sinister conspiracies buzzed about my brain. The next week I fixated on various people in the halls, an old high school classmate who had taken a dislike to me in grade nine but whom I hadn't really talked to since, a current classmate who occasionally looked at me (I thought) funny. Sometimes a voice, almost familiar, would indicate people, smirking hipsters in hallways in their grunge clothes and hair, old women on the sidewalk with feline eyes set in wrinkled skin. Those calls were an attack, a reminder that no one really wanted me, not awkward Telfryn Joncourt Tyde. But then they stopped. I nearly mentioned these events once, to the gaming group, but something prevented me. Kirt, to my knowledge, never brought it up again, and my brain settled.

We played our last game of the year at Brian's. Kirt's beefy brute, battling on unstable ground, had been knocked down by nothing more than the Barbed Devil's bristled tail and bumbled back down the brae. The dwarf I played, *Goœz Flagonmaster*, brandished battle axe against the beast. It hurled back flames and Brian rolled lucky on its behalf, doing dire damage to my already battered body. But Sonia's magic-bearing *Ursula*, and Augusta's warrior elf, *Augusta*, regrouped in a fatal two-flanked attack, sending it back to hell and acquiring the horde of items left by past, dead adventurers. The bronze dagger they found, Brian confirmed, was enchanted.

"The nature of the enchantment cannot yet be determined," he explained, as a battered Kirt clambered back up to the summit.

"You could be someone else next year," Augusta said to me, as Brian and I cleaned up the dishes.

I finished first year and found a summer job at a video store. My mother retreated further inside the house and herself. My father did a lot of yard work, and he tried to get me to watch the remainder of the hockey season with him. I still found rules regarding blues lines more confusing than *Monster Manual* statistics, and considered the tendency of Detroit fans to throw octopodes on the ice far more bizarre than anything *my* friends did.

I ran into Sonia at the start of the next year, before our first game night. We headed to a pub and grill near the mall, a place popular with students, where we drank too much in a dark corner booth. Once again she seemed genuinely interested, definitely flattered. She had been up late, completing her first paper, and she actually lay down on the bench, her head in my lap.

The waiter came around, started in with, *everything okay here* but smiled and changed midway to, *yeah I guess everything's okay here*. Sonia laughed, a little too loud. Augusta came in, smiled and waved, and came over to me. Her face dropped when she saw Sonia.

"Hey hon." Sonia staggered upright, looking uncomfortable. "I just had a bit too much to drink."

"Clearly," Augusta said. She sounded cold and imperious, which surprised me. I'd never known her to be puritanical.

Augusta and Brian started dating later that year: Brian who had waited, afraid to ask lest he disturb the universe and our friendship. Some months later, Sonia, frustrated following the break-up of a two-week fling with a rugby player, finally took up my offer. We grew into a relationship that mostly consisted of culinary experiments and awkward sex. Kirt grew more isolated and angry at our gaming sessions, fifth wheel on the wagon. His humor turned increasingly toxic, misogynistic gibes passing as edgy humor.

That summer, the four of us left Kirt behind and headed to our first World Science Fiction Con. We scraped together paycheques and pennies and headed to the City of Angels, which for us meant the convention hotel and a bonus two days at Disneyland. Augusta had visited the Mouse Kingdom as a girl, so she played tour guide. We splurged for a romantic dinner at the Blue Bayou where we gazed out on a virtual night and discussed the tech behind the Haunted Mansion and the socio-cultural implications of Tomorrowland as an actual future.

Sonia insisted we go to Venice Beach, which intrigued me, happy as I was once I found myself surrounded by bikinis and graffiti, sand sculptures and skates. A woman and an Indian elephant glided by on wheels. An aging hippie peddled from a pram. The place smelled of kelp and musk, pot and jasmine. We were unable to make the Ackermansion, the original, great SF collection, a forest of movie and genre memorabilia which still flourished at that time, but the con opened eyes to a wider world of thinkers and nerds. We shared a hotel room, which required a sensitivity that I could not always manage. I woke up the first morning to Brian and

Augusta's pale white bodies gambolling out of the shower.

Saturday afternoon Sonia tried to get me to a panel with someone called Takumi Shibano, not one of her manga heroes but someone who had translated a lot of English-language SF into Japanese. I declined, needing a power nap. I left Brian at a computer and tech workshop and crashed in the room. Augusta woke me up. She had bathed and she wore a white hotel towel.

"Nice outfit."

"Just put a little Enterprise symbol here, we'd have one of those old *Star Trek* uniforms—the miniskirt kind."

"Did they have white uniforms? Oh, maybe you're dressed for that *Next Gen* episode with the Planet of the Horny Blonds, you know, uh, where they jog around a Water Treatment Plant and have sex and try to kill Wesley Crusher?"

"Living the dream," she said. "Still, I think everyone has a part of their brain that would settle on that planet. A culture where everyone has sex without guilt?"

"O Brave New World, that has such people in it," I said, and she smiled and brushed her hair. I inhaled surf and jasmine again.

She sat down. It dawned on me I should leave to let her dress, but then she said, "We have common interests, Brian and me. And he was so reliable. The attraction came later. He's the kind of person you grow to like."

I nodded.

"We make too much of *involuntary* chemistry," she said. "Don't you think?"

"Brian's the most reliable of us."

She smiled. "I really meant it. When I called you. You know, those stupid flute serenades."

I paused and my brain tried to make sense of her words. "I didn't recognize your voice," I finally said.

She squinted her eyes and pushed her face forwards.

"Voices sound different on the phone, if you don't know who it is. I thought they were mocking me."

"What?"

"I couldn't believe... You were serious?"

"I'm sorry. And yes I was."

"Damn."

"You still like me?"

"Of course," I said. "Of course."

Her eyes widened and glowed, like something from the deep.

We dived in like a pair of chemical robots. I enjoyed my times with Sonia, though I never entirely understood her stranger requests. Later in my life, I had occasion with women who were willing, but until we started I never felt it mattered, one way or the other. I've never felt that overwhelming, unthinking passion for any specific person, except that once, in an Anaheim hotel room, with my hypothetical best friend's girlfriend. We washed and dressed hastily afterwards, terrified of the moment, and terrified for the door.

I closed my eyes and saw them, twin orbs that shifted from anthropoid to arthropod, each facet staring and accusing.

Sonia and Augusta stayed at the post-masquerade dance, late. I lost Brian in a labyrinth of crowds and drank too much at a succession of bid parties—one served up absinthe and another had an impossible machine near the bar, dials and gears and a computer screen and a ridiculous appliance that attached to the head and would *Reveal Your Inner Desires!* in random images from old monster movies and Japanese TV shows, all of which played for me in shades of green—stumbled down the halls feeling pursued and finally collapsed in our room, where I dreamed of Lovecraftian invertebrates with submarine eyes. My mouth tasted of licorice and herbs and battery terminals as I went under, and like the fur of a desiccated beast when I resurfaced. We returned to Ontario exhausted, and Sonia and I, noticeably cooler. I felt odd when she touched me. Kirt peered at our photos, said he was sorry to have missed the beach, but that Disneyland would only be worth it when they opened an audio-animatronic sex club. He didn't see the point of Augusta getting her copy of *The Diamond Age* autographed, especially as she had no plans to sell it, and absolutely railed at us for not getting into the Ackermansion. "Next trip," Brian said, decisively.

He found the roller-skating elephant and party tales slightly more interesting. "*Real* absinthe?" he asked, skeptically, and I assured him it had to have been.

Soon we were starting our first *real* jobs. Augusta and Brian announced their wedding date. "It has to be that way," she told me.

"I wouldn't say anything."

Brian's brother, whom he rarely mentioned, stood up for him. He explained, apologetically, that he had considered me, but Augusta thought he should become closer to his family.

Sonia was Maid-of-Honour.

She and I floundered and the gaming sessions grew awkward, when our cluttered schedules allowed us to hold them at all. Augusta no longer found Kirt tolerable, and complained vociferously about him when he was not around. Even his characteristic slouch seemed designed to put her off. The centre, clearly, could not hold.

Back home, my mother kept herself indoors, until finally, nothing my father or I could say could induce her to leave. He worked the yard and talked to neighbours, greeted people passing by, a familiar, lonely sight on the street. Over the years, they'd changed status from regular churchgoers to Christmas Christians, Easter visitors, and finally they dropped altogether. My father went once to seek solace; he was met with an unfamiliar matronly woman who had just been ordained. He left unadvised. Mother still read the Bible sometimes, sitting isolated in some corner of the house. She would ask child's questions, like what happened to the Wise Men's gifts, did Mary and Joseph use them as currency on the flight to Egypt? And did the Veil of the Temple tear in two before or after Jesus died? She would look into my eyes with terror and I would tremble.

I landed a job as a Process Operator in Chemical Valley. I held the cracks together in my own mind, until the year I turned twenty-seven. I'd find myself working among the stacks and tubes and metal grids of an alien city, the background in a Golden Age paperback cover. Voices would call for me around corners. The receptionist dropped references to her insectoid heritage, and the synthetic flesh unspooled from her spinnerets from which she daily spun her human disguise. My brain betrayed me, began sending reports and sensations into outer space. Thoughts from the crevices of my brain echoed in the world, and a foul scent began to follow me, like the smell that now permeated my parents' house. Brian and Augusta brought me to the hospital, all broken and jagged mind and nails. At first I wouldn't speak to them. Later, the odour disappeared as I resumed showering. The sinister cabal swirled down the drain with it, and I welcomed them back as friends—as, indeed, my saviours. The thing about being a delusional rationalist, any attempt to explain how the receptionist at work *could* be a clandestine arthropod breaks to pieces under even the most cursory analysis like a beetle crunched underfoot.

"She loves you," I told Brian, while Augusta went to get coffees. He looked at me like, *yeah, yeah, of course.*

I'm on a chemical regiment now that I need less and less as I age. I consume as many books as I like, from the library and friends and rummage sales. When I can save enough money, I join the tribe at one SF con or another, because they keep me sane. I see women and men I've known who remain in fandom, many, like me, heavy with midlife. But not Augusta, who for years has hiked and biked with her daughters. She still wears her dark hair long.

Augusta has aged better than any fangirl I know.

8

Lady Susan Vernon
The Constellation Inn
Friday

The journey from Lakefield to the metropolis was not beyond a few hours, and I set out without either dreading its length or feeling its solitariness. We arrived in Mississauga, and watched for the first appearance of the Constellation Inn with little perturbation; but when at length we turned in at the roundabout, my spirits were in a high flutter. The Constellation Inn is a large, brick-veneer building, standing well on paved ground, and backed by an expanse of scrubland and parking lots. I soon settled into comfortable lodgings, and changed into the costume and character more suited to the evening. I made a most grandiose entrance into our crowd. The chatter, hitherto most respectfully dedicated to her most esteemed wordsmith, by her dutiful and obedient humble readers, immediately turned their attention to my person. I received not a few compliments on the work, and to some I could return the compliment. A woman embroidered in her tambour frame. Two of the gentlemen present wore fine soldier's uniforms, with polished brass buttons. I should have lighted upon either such man, for I like a red coat very well; but, while I certainly greeted them both with convivial affection, my past experience has informed me they share lodgings year-round, and would share with the fairer sex only the most capricious and inconsequential of flirtations.

Denise Moon bestowed greetings upon me. She is perhaps thirty, round of face but with what I recollected as an amiable disposition. We first encountered each other one year ago, where we shared wine enough to raise our spirits and invite some confidence. I know that she harboured some melancholy about her life. Her parents wished her married and with family, as her older sister was, her older sister wished she would visit their parents more often, and she wished she possessed an apple-shaped bottom instead of the pear-shaped body that she acknowledged her own. She had notwithstanding a little beauty and when plied with wine and pressed could name some accomplishments. She possessed a charitable kindness that led her to assist with good works, mostly through a church she attended, and she assessed herself a fair cook, whether the occasion called for turkey casserole or Miyeok Guk. She was also an accomplished cellist. I turned our private conversation as quickly as decorum would merit to our situation in the hotel. The members of our party would be abed soon enough, it being their disposition to rest or read, and I hoped she would look favourably upon more wine, consumed not in our private quarters, as before, but that the large hotel and its bars should be the fairest field of action. "I think you should find many occasions for flirtation, and a little dissipation."

"Your dress," she remarks, "does shew a remarkable amount of cleavage for the period. I guess that suits your character. Oh, you're playing your character! Very good."

"It may be that I have chosen the character for a reason. Neither of us has grown any younger since our last encounter."

"My mother insists on how I'm too old to be unmarried, but I'm not desperate and I'm not looking for any sort of casual… Oh, I don't mean to judge."

Indeed, I think. It is very unfair to judge of any body's conduct, without an intimate knowledge of their situation. After proffering some excuse, I turned from my stammering companion. The tables featured tea and shortbread and apricot cakes—and sliced cantaloupe, which raised eyebrows and discussion among our fair assembly.

It is a wonder, of course, that anything that *we* might do should elicit surprise. Assembled here with us in the inn are the queerest folk as have ever decorated a map of an unknown land, imprinted in the distant past! At first glance of the lobby one observes only a crowd, though their manner of dress, at times, is strange. Many of the men sport garish shirts, and I spied at least three Scottish kilts and two American fedoras. As one takes a clear vantage, one realizes that, flitting among the crowd are found people with unexpected appendages, here and there ass's ears or cat's tails, and one or two creatures that barely seem human at all. I cannot help but wonder if suitable company might be found among these travellers from foreign stations. Indeed, a burly gentleman with whom I spoke earlier, though somewhat rough in his appearance, possessed a certain polish and charm. If adventures will not befall a lady in her own village, she must seek them abroad.

As the discussion over the syllabus for the morrow had been replaced with one concerning the presence of sliced cantaloupe, I resolved to look further afield for admirers of my Regency wear.

9
Con-Versation

The Slesaks have decided to dine in the consuite. The chili's the mild sort, which my gut can handle. Patti has taken a corner chair. Chelsea sits on the couch and Thomas has made certain he's got the spot next to her, leaving Mark to fight for a place. Brian and Augusta join me on the other side of the coffee table. An old fan, wizard-bearded, follows our conversation in silence. The room unreels like a movie. Brian asks if anyone else has seen the fish-creature costume, and I feel a chill I cannot explain, cold as the Kuiper Belt.

"Now *that's* a costume," says Thomas, looking at his brother's prosthetic Klingon forehead and fake novelty goatee.

"I know!" says Chelsea. "Like, how does that even work?"

"I was wondering if, uh, if it involves some mechanical effect. You know the face."

His brother concurs, in part. "Probably the face…"

"Those eyes."

"Yeah, but the whole thing can't be a robot."

"I guarantee that takes the masquerade," says Augusta. "Whatever it is."

"Anyone know what's it from?" asks Mark. No one can provide an answer, but those three-fingered hands claw at the back of my mind, things forgotten, kept uneasy in a vault with monstrous reptilian insects. We sit a moment, and eat. In hours, as I have said, I will know.

"What's worth going into the city for?" asks Thomas. "You girls are from here?"

"Yeah, if there's, if there's a big enough hole in programming," says Mark, self-consciously touching his latex forehead.

"We're from this town on Lake Huron," says Chelsea.

"Really!" Mark says. "We're from Holland. Holland, Michigan. So we're both… from coastal towns on the Great Lakes."

Thomas plays Obvious Captain Obvious, points out that, in fact, we're in the Great Lakes Basin, so if you tossed a Peeps candy in the air, the odds favoured the person stepping on it being from a coastal settlement on a Great Lake.

My chill having subsided, I gesture to Brian and Augusta. "These two know Toronto." Brian starts listing off some places, but Augusta notes that, this close to the airport, it's a bit of a hike to get to anything worth seeing but yes, did they know the city has one of the longest systems of publically-accessible underground tunnels in the world?

"Shiny," says Chelsea.

"The CN Tower," I say, pointing one finger skywards. A piece of high-toned Googie, it was dated before the plans dried, anachronistic by the time it and Augusta and Brian and I finally stood upright.

Augusta continues, flips back dark hair like she's one of the teenage girls. "Oh, now if you're going to go there, make lunch reservations. You get to skip the tourist line—"

"The restaurant has its own line," says Brian.

"—and the restaurant's above the observation deck." And from there we get the usual advice, that yes, you can walk down to the regular deck afterwards, but you'll have likely seen as much observation as you want and no, the food isn't that overpriced by big city standards and anyway you're paying for the view and then we start onto the Tower itself. I call it the tallest freestanding tribute to George Jetson and that faded postwar future. And then we're onto *The Jetsons*, which we all watched in reruns, a Space Age vision of our current century, with flying bubbletop cars and friendly robot servants. Lenticular houses sit, CN-tower-like, atop impossibly high pillars.

"Why don't we ever see the ground?" Brian and I ask, simultaneously, a fan-joke we've been sharing since we fought owlbears together around a Formica table. Augusta claps her hands and smiles and we're landing in California. We speak in double quotations.

"It could be a nuclear apocalypse down there."

"Environmental disaster run amok. Garbage and feral humans."

"Only the elite live in those elevated buildings."

"Gods help them if their bubblecars ever crash."

"Oh," says Chelsea. "This could like totally be a panel."

Mark the Klingon widens his eyes. It's so cute these young'uns haven't played this game before. "Zombie apocalypse. Seriously! No, see. *The Jetsons* and *The Walking Dead* coexist. The survivors are down there, and they're fighting zombies, and the elite are on the pole-buildings because the zombie virus doesn't reach up that high."

"So where are all the pillars in *Walking Dead*?" asks Thomas.

"It's just..." Mark trails off, looks for a moment like the environment will overwhelm him, the chips and Peeps and chili bowls foregrounded and his dialogue coming from some pathetic sketch in the distance. I look to Augusta whose face shows that she sees it, too.

I say, "I don't know what you grew up with. We still sort of believed in *The Jetsons* when we were kids." Brian and Augusta nod. "I mean, we thought the future would be space travel and flying cars. Instead we got autocorrect and Twitter."

"Sectarian religious wars and white supremacists," says Augusta, shaking her head.

"Our space stations don't even rotate," says Thomas.

"You have failed us," says Patti, scoping her elders accusingly. Chelsea cracks up. Patti looks over at Mark.

"Well," I say. "But we had all of those apocalyptic, Cold War and… environmental disaster stories. So it was a mix, even then." Science fiction hit the postwar pop culture as warning. Heinlein and Asimov may have been writing about engineering marvels and the harshness of real space travel, but the 50s movies gave us invading aliens. Then Hollywood held up apish reflections and dystopias with feathered hair. No wonder, I recall, looking at Mark's make-up, that *Star Trek* seemed a breath. We were going to the stars, and some aliens were downright friendly, even if others posed a threat. A logical balance, it must have seemed. Though my childhood featured *Trek* reruns, I discovered much of this later. By the time I was into the written stuff the media was serving up old-time heroes with light sabres. And an attempt to revive *The Jetsons* TV show with a new alien pet and references to floppy disks.

"I still," says Mark. "I stand by my zombie mash-up."

Thomas has a look of smug disapproval, but Patti says, "I'd watch that show."

"It'd be totally shiny." Chelsea removes her purple specs, hangs them on the v-neck of her top. Her eyes are bright, hypnotic.

Thomas smiles chess-masterfully, a man with a plan. Good for him, he thinks, if his brother connects with Patti. He makes eye contact with Chelsea Ashe. "So what are your plans for the con?"

"There's that one computer panel tomorrow—we're totally doing that. Oh, and we want to see that old guy who wrote for *Doctor Who*, old school *Doctor Who*. On that, like, *Doctor Who* panel? And there's that one tomorrow on contemporary folklore creatures, but it's opposite that one space science panel, so we"—she looks to Patti here—"may have to flip a coin or split up."

"That's good," says Mark, sounding inconsequential. But then he asks Patti about the space science panel, and they're talking, and Mark's himself again. He plays much better as himself. I can almost ignore the prosthetic forehead. He takes a sudden conversational U-turn. "Two people walking behind each other?" he asks, repeating the same thought I'd had in the elevator. I shiver again.

"They'd have to be so little. Like kids or dwarves," says Chelsea. "Acrobats."

"Side by side, I think," Patti says. "One operates an arm on each side. The other arms do the face." She mimes a puppet with one hand. "But that's so complicated," Patti says.

"It looks epically shiny."

"You could still use some kind of robotics in the arm. Like, for the, for the hands, the digits."

"Those *were* very long arms," Patti says. Chelsea illustrates her friend's comment, stretching her arms out, like a thing in a rerun monster-movie.

"At this rate," Augusta says, "it would be easier to just hire a real alien." Her husband laughs, a laughter bordering on his old bray.

"It's CGI," says Patti. She picks up her Solo cup and sips.

During the laughter I escape my thoughts by wondering what Denise Moon might be doing and if I should seek her out and apologize, when I look up and see Lady Susan Vernon standing in the consuite door.

10
Kate Meets the Doctor at an Electric Hoedown

Kate finds herself back in the lobby, frustrated with herself, after cruising the con and trying to find Chelsea. She contemplates her cell phone. The last ding was home. If she has to, she'll contact Chelsea directly, explain that she is here, in town—the rational thing to do, if anything here were rational—but she can wait until tomorrow, after her tour and some quality time with Aunt Izzy and Uncle Phil. She intends to make her way back just then, but she hears the rhythmic *oonth oonth oonth* and follows it to the Friday dance, underattended but lively. Chelsea likes to dance, and surely she can't pass every beat of the con with her bestie. Kate takes a deep breath of air and a drink from the fountain, sets her bag by the blue-skinned attendant at the door, and scans the floor.

Three girls, maybe college age, dance in a group. The short-haired one, unless Kate's detection skills have gone off from teen years of repression, has a thing for the pink-haired girl with cat ears. They dance, lean in, chatter. The third girl, bleach-blonde and great legs, wears a dark skirt and what looks like a man's formal shirt with sleeves removed. She sports a red bowtie with matching suspenders and fez, waves around some kind of techno-magic wand. I would have recognized the cosplay right away; it is only in the right flash of light that Kate sees clearly, and recalls the girl from the lobby. Finally, the phrase *sonic screwdriver* comes to mind, activating memories of hanging at Chelsea's two weeks earlier and trying to make sense of *Doctor Who.*

The Doctor does a double take and then whispers something to the others. They're looking without looking like they're looking, and Kate suddenly feels *vulnerable*, and then angry with herself. She stares down opponents without effort. But she knows in that instant *why* they're looking. She feels it. Then the Doctor dances her way to the sidelines, like, "*hai!* Do you wanna dance?" Emotionally tired and frustrated and away from anyone from the team or the locker room or the Rose Point Challenge, she takes the hand of the girl who offers it. Besides, the Doctor might know Patti and Chelsea, or have a clue where they'd be.

"Katie," she says, and then, "Kate." She bumps the Doctor's other hand, bro-like. The girl wears a sleeveless tee, she realizes, the tie and suspenders printed on. The headgear is real, though, and the Doctor's face runs sweaty when she tips her fez.

"I'm looking for someone."

"Oh?" queries the Doctor, who should probably never play poker.

Kate smiles. "It's complicated."

"It's always complicated, Miss Katie. We could just go for a walk. My friends... It's the dance, and I don't wanna be their third wheel, you know?" They step closer to the door.

"You might know her. Chelsea? Chelsea Ashe?"

The Doctor shakes her head. "I don't think so. She like your girlfriend? If I can ask." It's supposed to sound private, between sisters, but they're both yelling at close range to be heard above the beat the *oonth* the synth mix.

She takes a deep breath. "I don't know."

"Let's talk. We have some coolers in our room."

"I'm not a drinker."

"Maybe you wanna start?" She waves the sonic screwdriver. It whirs and winks. By then they're at the door, where the blue-skinned security—Kate realizes he also sports fake-looking deely-bobbing antennae—talks to, apparently, Thor. They walk to the faux leather chairs in the lobby and sit; the Doctor removes her fez and mops sweat from her forehead, then baptizes both with a little water from her plastic bottle.

She sees Kate staring at the blue man. "Andorian,"

she says. "He's an Andorian. From *Star Trek*. So you're looking for this girl and you haven't texted her?"

"She doesn't know I'm here. *Here.*" She gestures to the Andorian and the Norse God across the way. "Yet."

"Ah…"

"She said I should come to this con." She had, too, because after that day on the beach, they returned to the Ashe place, but everyone was home, retreating from the heat, and so they watched *Doctor Who*, and then Chelsea had told her about the con at summer's end. "She and her friend Patti. Maybe you know Patti? She has cerebral palsy, walks with this sort of twisty leg hobble thing?"

"Yeah. Yeah. I've seen *her*."

"When?"

"About an hour ago."

"Oh."

"With some other people."

"Was there a hot girl with purple glasses?"

"Yes! Most definitely."

"That's Chelsea."

"Wow."

Kate smiles, recalls being baffled by *Doctor Who*, and then how Chelsea managed enough time alone and they kissed, one brief and terrific kiss.

"Ah. You know, I think they were with a pair of boys."

Kate says nothing.

"Probably just going to the same panel." She lets a beat pass. The Doctor and Kate smile at each other. Each sees something about the other that invites confidence, and they talk. The Doctor and her friends, she learns, have just graduated high school.

"I mean, Chelsea's a friend."

The Doctor raises an eyebrow.

"We hang out. I... It's difficult. We have some kids who are out and like that, but..." I mean, what's the point in not just saying it now? "Small town. You guys were out at school?"

"Of course." The Doctor does a double blink. "Really, Miss Katie? No one suspects?"

"People see what they want to see. We hang out. It's there but it's not there."

"But here you are, in Toronto."

"Okay. Here I am. I'm going to check out U of T with my aunt tomorrow. And, maybe, you know, see Chelsea. Away from the Point. Our town."

"Uh-huh."

"People need to do these things in their own time."

"People need to do these things."

"Obviously, Doctor, you've never been a small-town lesbian."

She laughs, a laugh of recognition. "But it might cost you this Chelsea chick."

"If that's even ever going to be a thing."

"So, technically, you're single right now. I mean, I'm just saying. Just putting it out there."

"Is there a place people are likely to be?"

"The dealers' room. The consuite, especially in the morning. You know, at meals?" She looks at Kate's face. "This looks effed up to you, doesn't it?"

Kate nods. The other two join them. Introductions go around and she's sure, as she retrieves her bag, that one or both of the companions give the Doctor a thumb's up behind her back. The blue man nods at the group, some of his makeup running, revealing the pink flesh beneath. At this point maybe Kate will even try one of those goshawful coolers. The Doctor does most of the talking as they walk away, and Kate wonders if she's being offered what she thinks she's being offered and is it just that easy for some people. About then I see Kate for the first time. We don't know each other yet, but I pass them, led by Lady Susan.

Kate first met Chelsea in grade nine. Actually, Chelsea met Sara, part of Kate's squad since, maybe, kindergarten. Sara and Chelsea worked together in English. Their presentation recast the story of Persephone as a Dr. Phil family intervention and achieved mythic status in the class. A few days later Chelsea found herself lounging around the rec room in a house at the end of Elmwood Ave: pizza, *Mario Party*, and impressions of high school. Sara got on with Chelsea; both are prone to giggling and random commentary.

"We're real athletes," she insisted, when her friends called her on cheerleading. "With trophies and everything." And Chelsea, whose sporting life consisted of *World of Warcraft*, championed Sara's claim. Brianna held back; the girl in the purple glasses was far too strange, like, she hangs with that Patti girl and the Tech Club nerds.

Kate tried on the shades. "Purple anchovies," she said, looking at her pizza slice. "How do you even *see* in these?"

"I know, right?" Chelsea laughed, hysterically, shifting on the broad leather sofa. "The world looks awesome in purple." She had an infectious charm and moved like a natural dancer. She was different from Kate's friends, though Kate then still hadn't *quite* embraced the possible, particular nature of that difference. But, as they drifted back into their disparate groups—much to Brianna's approval—Kate never forgot their first encounter. The hack back in autumn? Kate was the first to cast an approving eye to Patti and Chelsea. *It had to be them*, said with assurance and sassy smile, a glance askance with raised eyebrow.

We can take as gospel that Kate calls Aunt Izzy and clears staying overnight, and her aunt takes the request as good news and is, in fact, grinning conspiratorially on the other end, Kate can just tell. *This con thing is huge, I just thought and yeah I look forward to the tour, I can't wait to see you Auntie... And Uncle Phil. Give hugs to him and the cats.*

She finds the room comfortably beige, and insists for the umpteenth time she'll sleep on the floor. She peruses her copy of the program, trying to determine what panels or workshops would most likely draw Chelsea. "I *am* still looking for her," she says, as the Doctor undresses for bed. "That's why I'm here."

"I know. I wasn't going to *not* meet you, though. So here we are. We'll find your Chelsea chick tomorrow." She's changing into an outsized TARDIS tee now. On the bedside table rests, not the expected SF novel or manga, but a copy of I *Heard the Owl Call My Name.*

"See. I'm here. I'm away from home. And I'm going to finally just tell her."

"All right Kate!"

She inhales sharply. "I worry I'm gonna lose friends. We're there, but we're not there." Her school has a small GSA, but the team might not want her in the locker room. The old insults still fly back home, the guys in particular, like, *he's up for MVP? I could see him getting an award for sucking the most cock, har dar.*

"Kate?"

"Yeah?"

"Those friends you're gonna lose?"

"Yeah."

"They aren't your friends."

But they are, Kate thinks. The last thing she removes are the hairbands she keeps around her wrist (a game may break out at any moment; she needs to be able to restrain her brown hair) and at some point, she falls into sleep and dreams she walks through a desert wilderness. Perhaps she meets a hooded creature, like an upright fish with four legs and two long arms and large, keen eyes. It sweeps out its left arm and fans the three fingers of its hand. And before her, Kate sees a cheering crowd of fangirls, sports fangirls, and they're interested and she doesn't need to explain to them that a free throw is only worth one point when you score. None of them have heard of Ursula K. Le Guin or Robert Charles Wilson or Lauren Beukes and they don't care how many actors have played the Doctor and whether or not Peter Cushing counts.

The next morning, the girls prepare a breakfast of caffeinated macaroni and cheese in a rice cooker. Afterwards, the companions return to bed. Kate and the Doctor—now the tenth, rather than the eleventh Doctor—same skirt, a Sally Ann striped suitcoat over a lacy bra, and aggressively nerdy glasses—head into the hall. The Doc insists on hugging Kate goodbye and wishing her luck—

—just as Patti and Chelsea come down the hall.

11
Telfryn Joncourt Tyde: Secret Origins II

We attended the Anglican Church regularly in my childhood. When I thought about the Gospel readings, I imagined the four evangelists playing reporter and nailing down the facts in interviews with, say, Joseph the Carpenter and the Centurion whose daughter was cured. But who overheard what Jesus said in Gethsemane whilst the disciples slept? And did He mention, perhaps over dinner conversation, one night, about that one time, when Satan tempted him in the wilderness? How much guidance did the Holy Ghost provide, providing whole details, or divinely editing the copy? How many of Denise Moon's fellow parishioners accept those stories without bothering to ask?

Perhaps all religion starts as a cargo cult, making sense of things seen and heard but imperfectly understood: an alignment of stars at Solstice, a voice on the Road to Damascus, a headset on Melanesia. Narrative and fanfic come later. We shape character and setting into meaning, attribute wisdom or folly, good or evil. I don't know where the ritual fits in, the LARPing, the Live Action Role-Playing. I would say it comes last, but other perhaps wiser heads have proffered other perhaps wiser arguments.

People con themselves, move mountains to support the literal truth of a global flood or the divinity of Prince Philip, the alien origins of Puma Punku or the honour in killing an unchaste daughter. God tells them to continue old Pagan and cultural rituals, because it turns out, they were doing the right thing all along, just in the name of the wrong deity. Others forego literality and hunt for symbol and metaphor, while imitating structures and forms they find comforting and meaningful. They may act in accordance with ancient myth and scripture or they may devote a part of their life to George Lucas or Jane Austen.

I look back on my own life and see perception coalesce into story: the Dog Star, the Christmas Stumbo died, and a passing moment outside his funeral.

I met Gregory Stumbo in the days when my medication still required frequent adjustment. A fallen Baptist who used to mistake his delusions for heavenly visions, he was disturbed enough that people felt genuinely menaced. I grew my beard, which was already graying, and we'd go drinking from questionably clean glasses at the Dog Star. Underlit in yellow, we looked like desperate men. The place occasionally gave me a sex life, aging honktonk honeys who through the filter of alcohol found me cute. The Slesaks tried to discourage me from going. Brian would shake his head, laugh with a muted bray. I accepted assistance from the Slesaks, when it came, but felt so unworthy, for I had been the silent serpent, as I saw it, in their Eden.

The Dog Star proved a judgment.

In December a fight broke out in the parking lot between groups of guys over a dinged car door. Within, the décor still consisted of torn Naugahyde and brewery giveaways, but they'd hung old holiday lights above the bar and set a saturnine Santa near the entrance. His plastic cap was missing and the paint on his face had worn. Stumbo and I stumbled out before closing and I started heading home. He went in the back of the parking lot to get a hot dog. A sallow vendor there sold year round and in the most appalling weather. And then the fight began. No one had a gun, but there was a glass bottle and buckle-ended belts and one hunting knife. Three outnumbered two and one of the two had been Stumbo's roommate in the psych ward, years ago. As the two swung their belts and tried to keep the three at bay, Stumbo grabbed one—the one, as it turned out, with the hunting knife. He took it to his heart and died in the lot, splatterpunked, body in blood just like a late night movie or an old ballad. I stumbled back too late to help. Three fled in a small car, possibly an old Ford Escort. They have never been identified, and the witnesses provided four different licence plates. No one knew them, apparently—out of towners who hit the 402, cruising drunk, streets not straight—into darkness.

I never returned. The place closed the following summer, and it remains a boarded-up, burned-over eyesore from which the police roust transients and addicts and urban spelunkers. But in the wake of that awful moment I experienced no full-blown episode, either. When I stepped outside from Stumbo's funeral, attended by his mostly-estranged family and myself and Augusta, who drove me, I took in cold December air and sky and tried to feel as much warmth as I could from the sun. I'd had nights of uneven sleep and frightened tremors but my sanity did not slip. She had parked at a far end of the lot, which struck me as odd because there were plenty of spots and she was then pregnant with Maya.

We stood in December sun across the street from a white wooden house and talked a bit and I hugged her, held her close. A passer-by said, out of nowhere, "hey, cut it out! How do you think she got that way?" I felt my heart go warm and then miss a beat and we met eyes and I felt lightened by the weight of lives I'd never lead. I will recall that hug forever; I felt closer to her than when we'd fucked.

And still I remained sane.

I ate Christmas dinner with the Slesaks, in a dining room Norman Rockwell might have painted, Grandma fussing over little Miranda, and Brian wielding the utensils on the turkey. The careful viewer would see the lemon-seed on the window-sill, planted in an old *Star Trek* Ferengi mug. Augusta's parents asked me, didn't I know the victim? Didn't I go to *that* place sometimes? Was it about drugs? I tried, apologizing that, really, I witnessed nothing. I described the setting, and the bar; the rest I said I'd mostly gleaned from conversation and coverage. Augusta's mother blinked and shook her dyed head. I thought of her daughter, of the pavement and the December sun and a pregnant belly against me.

12

Lady Susan Vernon
The Constellation Inn
Friday Evening

Like most of the Janeite company, Miss Denise Moon is conservative in her nature, but I hitherto believed that accompanying this nature was a levity of spirit that might compel her to join me in seeking adventures and flirtations. Her impudent comment, however a product of a tired and unthinking mind, belies my previous opinion of her. She retired to her room and I suppose we shall be civil tomorrow, and perhaps even friendly. I enjoy our discussions altogether too much.

I rather fancied the tenor who sang "Robin Adair" for us. Alas, he departed soon thereafter, no doubt resting himself for his part in tomorrow's Evensong. I moved onward. A hotel of this size and in the metropolis affords an unattached woman a field for adventures not so easily found in the lakeside counties.

A public notice posted on a wall provided the information I sought, and I followed the hubbub and revelry to the Consuite of the Science Fiction folk. My confident manner and brightly-hued historic garb, with its elegantly-detailed work, meant that no one questioned my presence, despite my lack of proper certification. The overseer was a person of perhaps five and thirty years, with a coiffure as brightly coloured as my dress, tresses of purple and blue and crimson. People called this person Paul or Paulie, but never Paula, but, be it gentleman or lady, Paulie must be most competent to manage such a crowd as this.

I recognized in the consuite the man I had met earlier in the elevator. He must have been quite handsome in his younger years and, even now, though he has gained perhaps too much in the way of weight and wrinkles, he remains attractive, and has acquired a rugged patina that suggests he has led a most interesting life. He had impressed me earlier with his knowledge of my identity—with the knowledge, indeed, of Miss Austen's work at all, an accomplishment I had not expected from one of his peculiar associations. Only later would I understand the assistance he had received that allowed him to divine my name.

A young serving-girl cleared the table as I entered, replacing the empty dishes with food both sweet and savoury, including "Cheese Doodles." They met with the approval of an old whitebeard, who partook of them, somewhat gluttonously. Cheese powder fell from his mouth as he ate, flecking his generous whiskers.

Mr. Telfryn Joncourt Tyde reintroduced himself, more formally than on the occasion of our first meeting. He next presented me to his acquaintances and travelling companions, a Mr. and Mrs. Slesak, a handsome, if eccentric couple. Mr. Slesak is a smallish man, though he has kept himself in fair condition. I grant him the pleasure of laughter, but it must be said, his laugh itself I found ever so slightly annoying. These limitations aside, he nevertheless exuded some air of command. He was not born with it, I am sure, but acquired it, and its use put a stress upon him. His wife's form was more athletic than her husband's and, in having the advantage of height, was also more striking. Her hair was brown in colour, and worn long. Both Slesaks must have witnessed the passing of forty years, but might have been mistaken for five and thirty. We spoke for a short time, in which they expressed a keen interest in my costume. Too soon they excused themselves from our company. They had plans to attend a lecture on how the virtual worlds of gaming and social networks have influenced our concept of identity, and how these trends have been reflected in the contemporary literature, including the novels of Mr. Charles Stross.

"You must join us, later, at the Starlight Lounge," said Mr. Slesak. I took no umbrage at their departure; indeed, it left me with fewer competitors for the attentions of Mr. Telfryn Tyde. I could not but notice, however, upon their departure, a most peculiar backward glance by the robust and healthy Mrs. Slesak.

We were not to remain long under the hospitality of Mistress? Mister? Paulie. Telfryn inquired as to the business of the Society, and I provided some description of what had transpired earlier that evening. After some pleasantries, he said, "You might enjoy this panel I'm going to next."

"I'm intrigued," I replied. "What's the matter of the panel?"

"Writing Effective Alternate History. Our two big-name guests are on it. They both have a superlative understanding of history."

"I fancy I shall take you up on your offer and see how I fare. I trust you're not too scandalized?"

He offered me his arm and so we left. Whitebeard forbore his circumstances, consoling himself with additional Cheese Doodles. The consuite is a busy place, and I am informed that convivial beverages soon would be made available. He knew he would not for long remain alone!

13
Plot Conventions

Chelsea noticed Patti first, walking past the playground, as Chelsea sat fearlessly atop the slide, the big metal slide with the painted fish on its sides. Patti held her mother's hand, or perhaps her grandmother's, that little girl who moved like nobody else. Chelsea wondered if she'd hurt her leg, somehow. Their friendship started with that question, just natural curiosity. They got to know each other, and the Ashe family provided another home for Patti, who was otherwise shunted between mother and grandparents. Patti and Chelsea would take their toys on fantastic adventures, exploring distant realms around their yards, alien landscapes in dirt. Barbie conquers the Universe! They watched videos and played video games and sketched their perfect home, which was also a spaceship. Eventually, they made their way back to the playground, with its towering slide, and that flat cartoon fish decorating either side.

Chelsea helped her up the ladder that challenged her twisted movement and shook her confidence. And Patti slid down the slide, to the bottom, just like every other kid. Most of the time, after that, she got back up the ladder by herself, though she made slow progress and avoided it when others were about. A boy mocked her once, told her to move her butt. It's possible Patti put that aside, but Chelsea never did.

They read *A Wrinkle in Time* and it opened the portal to more challenging works. The stars were soon their destination. They began to tinker with reality in computers and sound and light. Got together to watch each new episode of *Doctor Who* and compared the American and Japanese edits of *Sailor Moon*. The years passed and there had been others—a boy Chelsea dated in grade nine, a girl she flirted with in ten, and then, Kate. There would be others, but there would always be Patti and Chelsea, the rock of friendship.

Kate the Athlete hugging a female Doctor, first thing Saturday morning? Chelsea may be shocked, but Patti is poised to strike.

"Chelsea!" Of course. Kate imagined herself freshly showered, returned from U of T, bold, ready to take Chelsea's hand and walk through her world. She recovers, and introduces the Doctor.

"The famous Chelsea," says the Doctor, but she looks cornered, which is not at all helpful.

"Kate?"

"You invited me. I wanted to surprise you."

She eyes the Doctor. "You have."

Kate's distracted a minute by Chelsea's Star Wars tee-shirt, the chisel-featured Han Solo: *You like me because I'm a scoundrel.* "We met last night."

"Oh?" queries Patti.

"I did sleep here," explains Kate. "See, I'm... visiting my aunt and uncle. You know, my Aunt Izzy?"

Chelsea has put the tinted glasses back on, shields back up.

"I'm going to tour U of T. But it was late. I was tired... There's three of them—it wasn't like that! The three of them—I couldn't find you and I met the three of them, and they offered me a place, and it was easier than going back to my aunt and uncle's. You invited me. And I came to find you."

"It's too bad they haven't invented a way for us to, like, contact each other." As Chelsea says this she produces her cell phone.

"Care for breakfast?" asks the Doctor. "There's some mac and cheese left over in the room."

"I wanted to surprise you. I'm here in your world. Because... You know, this is a little public, Chels. Maybe we could...?"

"It's caffeinated."

"I'll have some," says Patti, but she still eyes the young woman with suspicion. The Doctor steps into her room.

"It's always *public*, isn't it? Gods forbid anyone should know..." The cell phone dings.

Patti—somewhat irritated—takes Chelsea's cell

and replies to Thomas's text.

The Doctor returns with a bowl of the caffeinated mac and cheese and hands it to Patti, who returns Chelsea's cell. And then the Doctor takes a breath and says, "You guys went to the beach a couple weeks ago and then you went to your house and she really wanted to... *say* something but your whole family was there and so you watched *Doctor Who*. But then you kissed goodnight."

They look at her.

"Why would she tell me that unless she was putting up a large honkin' stop sign? If she wasn't totally fixated? Feel for me, people. My friends in there are all over each other and I meet a hot girl and all she wants to do is talk about some girl she's not even really dating yet. She followed you to Toronto, Miss Chelsea. She's fuckin' crazy about you."

The frame freezes. A moment later, the scene continues. Kate—she moves with grace and care—steps closer. She wasn't expecting an audience for their second real kiss, never mind a young woman dressed as the protagonist of the longest-running SF series in history giving them a bittersweet *awww*! The geometric pattern on the carpet, reminiscent of early computer graphics, and the fluorescent lights spin like galaxies, and then Katie, who knows how to keep balance, says, "Look. Let's see your con. I have to tour U of T..."

"Perhaps you'll see my father," says Patti.

"But that can be later. It could be Sunday… I came for *you*."

"Me?" Somehow, Chelsea's eyes grow even larger.

"You."

A second, prolonged, kiss later, they step back.

"Well then," says the Doctor, smiling.

Two familiar young men come down the hall. Mark has become human. His forehead bears red marks from the extra-special ridges he had glued on the night before. He's cute, Patti thinks, with the fake goatee removed and, for all his insecurity, in better shape than his older brother. His actual hair is a kind of shaggy boy cut, locks and licks in different directions, but strangely artful, rather like his brother's coif, also an artistic straight-out-of-bed look, though Thomas's consists more of thick curls.

"Hey," says Thomas, pointing to Chelsea. "You're still wearing my shirt."

14

Lady Susan Vernon
The Constellation Inn
Friday Night

Such adventures for the first day!

On Mr. Telfryn Tyde's arm I gained easy access to the panel, despite the absence of what my escort called a "Con Badge."

"They probably think you're someone from *The Diamond Age*," he said. "Or *The Difference Engine*." The selection of titles makes no difference to me. Although I regard myself as educated, I am unfamiliar with these particular works of literature. "Yes. Put on some goggles and you could be a steampunker." I smiled, uncertain if I desired an explanation for that term. The discussion grew lively, for one held late in the evening, and I surprised myself by following so very many of the ideas under consideration. I learned the term *Jonbar Point*, taken from the writings of Mr. Jack Williamson, and we considered such things as how the death of one man in the 1940s might have led to a Jewish homeland in Alaska. Our personal lives too, they wryly observed, fill with such Jonbar Points. Decisions made one day, even as regards seemingly inconsequential matters, take on significances and the paths we take might be very different as a result.

"If you leave here and go to bed," said the discussion's moderator, "or if you leave here and have a drink—well, we leave you each at that Jonbar Point."

We inclined to meet with Mr. and Mrs. Slesak in the Starlight Lounge.

A performer crooned "Lost in the Stars" as we gazed out on the lights of the metropolis which indeed resembled a vast expanse of night sky. The waitress brought a round of cocktails and, though I most wanted an orange and raspberry shrub, I felt uncertain they would have such a drink and, rather than face disappointment and, following the suggestion of our hosts, who insisted upon paying, I instead imbibed a Moon Shot. Telfryn partook of a beer, as suited his rough exterior. I noticed that he limited himself to a single pint. The assembled crowd seemed better and more conventionally dressed than in the Suite, though here and there one saw tee-shirts promoting past SF gatherings and popular entertainments, and many sported con badges. More astounding was the movement of leaves and spines, as a most extraordinary pair of plants entered the room. Augusta identified these as Triffids, a perennial favourite. Fantastic as these beings were, the marvellous nature of the evening would be heightened with a new, and unexpected guest, present due to a decision that our esteemed panellists could no doubt discuss at length as an example of a Jonbar Point.

I noticed Mr. and Mrs. Slesak gazing at me rather intently, and wondered as to their aim. "Your costume," the woman finally asked. "Did you make it yourself?" On this topic I had much to say, and permitted the handsome woman and her husband to examine its finer details, she being rather inclined to run fingers along fabric.

Denise Moon had confided in me a year earlier that she oft encountered difficulties sleeping the first night in a strange environment. Furthermore (I do suspect) she may have felt goaded by my earlier comments on her recalcitrance towards enjoying the many tastes of life. Perhaps she just desired to see this other world, since our own events would transpire during the weekend proper. Her reasons, in the end, are her own—but whatever they were, they brought her, at that late night, dressed and washed, up to the Starlight Lounge just as we made our first toast. We caught sight of each other's eyes as she stood by the bar (where sat a third costumed individual, this one disguised with the head and single hand of a common fly), casting her gaze about the lively assemblage.

Social convention demanded she approach us to speak awhile, but I felt surprised by the forcefulness with which she approached, combined with an expression of bewilderment. "Telfryn?" she asked. The looks of surprise on our faces doubtless would have pleased the crowds at Drury Lane.

"Do you know each other, then?" I asked.

"We do," she said, though for the moment she declined further comment.

Telfryn raised a glass in a silent toast.

"But Miss Moon," I said, a wry look upon my face. "I left you preparing for your night's slumber. Whatever are you doing in this tavern?"

She said she had come only to have a quick drink, claiming, indeed, a difficulty falling asleep. "I don't get to places like this," she said, an ingenuous look upon her round face. "Normally. I don't want to interrupt you, of course." I saw her eyes fall briefly on Telfryn. Was it just surprise, then, at seeing him here? I took in again his rugged handsomeness, aged, but also refined in the crucible of a life fraught with challenges.

"Please," said Mr. Brian Slesak, extending his arm. "Join us."

"The more the merrier," said his wife. He responded with a brief laugh, almost becoming an asinine crow, but he stifled it, so as to retain an appearance of sophistication more in keeping with the tone of his surroundings. The waitress arrived about that point, drawn by the pull of a new customer.

"Would you like a Moon Shot?"

"Is that a drink?"

Collectively, we nodded.

"A Moon Shot would be appropriate," noted Telfryn, who thus won for himself a small round of laughter.

"Is it strong?"

We nodded again.

"Perhaps just… Do you have mead?"

The waitress smiled. "We do," she said. "We hardly ever serve it and you're the fifth one tonight!" After a short time, Miss Moon had her order.

"I blame the travel," said Miss Moon. "I never sleep comfortably the first day in a strange bed."

"I know what you mean," said Mrs. Slesak, with just a hint of suggestion in her voice.

Miss Moon turned to me. "So how did you meet Telfryn?"

"The inn is not *so* very large."

"She joined a discussion in the consuite. It's a suite for people at the SF con. Then she came with me to a panel."

"So blame it on chance," I said.

"It was a panel on alternate history."

"It all sounds very trivial," said Miss Moon.

15
The Altrusians vs the Extraordinary Legion of Über-Pwners

Blame the killer robots.

That summer, Chelsea acquired her G1 driver's licence. She immediately took Patti for a drive. Chelsea's dad, as required, rode shotgun. They made slow progress around town, down Shoreline Road and then up the hill, downtown, and through the Jiffy Car Wash. Chelsea came prepared for the passage of spray and foam. She found the correct place on her playlist and they heard the Star Gate chorus from 2001: A *Space Odyssey*, the angel voices and devil horns that accompany Astronaut Bowman's journey through a numinous canal to be born again as the Starchild. Mr. Ashe rolled his eyes and then chortled appreciatively. The girls discovered much on their own, but Chelsea's dad had introduced them to old *Star Trek*—Klingons and Vulcans and space adventures with moral lessons—and some classic SF films and novels. They read their way through his collection and watched *Space Odyssey* when their friends were still fixated on *Spongebob* and *Hannah Montana*. He also had the complete *Land of the Lost* on DVD, a misplaced piece of his own childhood, and they watched the family of explorers parry with low-budget reptilian Sleestaks and Altrusians and gambol with Grumpy the Tyrannosaurus.

Patti's mother had forced herself to become a do-it-yourselfer, and encouraged Patti in the same direction. The girls spent time in her basement workshop, too, though their interests soon changed to tinkering with computers.

Patti's father lives in Toronto.

Short version: Charlotte Washington is brilliant, but she was at one time not worldly. She left for school and fell for her young physics professor. She called him quirky then; now we'd call it mild autism spectrum disorder. He called it quits when he realized what a wife and family would entail. Charlotte kept Patti and moved back to the Point. The Professor sends money. In Patti's memory, she learned to walk before she met him, and she took a few years to learn to walk. Her mother swears he stopped by earlier, she just doesn't recall.

At puberty Patti discovered boys, but kept her feelings mostly to herself, because boys were transparent and annoying. When Chelsea discovered her attraction to *people*, Patti frankly wished she had the option.

They leave the consuite Friday night and people walk past between late-night panels and the masquerade dance. And there are the boys again. Thomas, smiling, asks the girls if they know anything about killer robots.

"We built a robot, once," Chelsea says.

"Really."

"It wasn't the killer kind, though," Patti adds, a note of regret in her voice.

"Robotics club," says Chelsea.

"Our robot had to sort and stack."

"Recycled stuff."

"I bet it was, it was good," says Mark.

"It was. We had the most awesome stack of recyclables in three counties."

"We did that robot team in high school," says Thomas. "I'm in electrical engineering now at U of Michigan. Ann Arbor."

Mark says. "I start there in September."

"Great town. You should visit. I'm going to be living with my irritating brother."

"Me too. Me too."

"Yeah, fem engineering, is it, bro? Sorry, *chem* engineering?"

Patti frowns.

"It's just a joke. For some reason that's the one type of engineering that attracts a lot of women."

"Well, maybe," Mark says. "I'm... I was the top mark in chemistry. Which naturally that makes me an incredible chick magnet."

Mark reminds Patti a little of Steve, she realizes, minus the confidence, with messier hair and interests. The Klingon forehead and beard, for example.

"Isn't there a dance?" he asks. "Oh..."

"Chelsea likes to dance. Me not so much."

Thomas throws him a glance, and then says, "Hey, bought this." He unfolds the shirt he carries in his tote bag, a Han Solo *Empire Strikes Back* tee, smelling of fresh ink: *You like me because I'm a scoundrel.* "Whereas this guy..." And Mark has already reached into his tote bag, producing a whitish cotton robe.

"It's..."

"Overpriced."

"It's the Vulcan robe Spock wears in *The Voyage Home*."

"So sometimes you're a Vulcan?" asks Chelsea.

"Not so far, but... it's perfect for lounging. I can wear it around our apartment next year..."

"The ladies will just be throwing their panties at our window," says Thomas.

"As ladies do," says Patti.

Chelsea laughs, and then asks, "So where to?"

"Well, if you know about robots..." Thomas says. "Have you ever heard of the Yoshimites?"

"Yoshimites?" Chelsea asks.

Thomas smiles at them. This con has been full of surprises, and they have to give him credit for uncovering this one, because it's not in the program.

They're duking it out in an obscure corner of the hotel's parking garage, a place which pretty much fits the reputation of such structures, what the *New York Times* called "the grim afterthought of American design." I didn't read that there; the article gets quoted anytime someone feels the need to write about parking garages. Brutalist concrete underlit with fluorescent squares, dirt; pylons of orange and gold set the borders of the arena, around which the slight group of competitors and spectators circumambulate and settle uncomfortably. Most of these geeks know each other from the legitimate robo-competitions, but they like the underground thing, with its dearth of rules and safety. The Yoshimites advertise by word of mouth and text: too much popularity and suddenly the frat bros and corporate types want in and then you're just another Burning Man.

The brothers and the girls examine crowd and tech and concrete. Mark felt comfortable in spaces such as these.

Two groups have brought homemade 'bots. Each side does last-minute tweaks. Thomas, Mark, Chelsea, and Patti join the furtive group and try to determine what each robo-gladiator can do. A few people nod appreciatively at Mark's costume, a little worse for wear but still holding together with honour. Mark asks Patti about their stacking-and-sorting bot, because dammit if their small-town team doesn't sound infinitely more advanced than anything the one at his school managed.

"Do you know about chemical robots?" he asks.

"How biopunk. Tell me more." But then one of the robots spins and shows its narrow end.

"Is that a flame thrower?" Mark asks.

"Looks like it," Patti says. "Not necessarily effective against a metal robot."

"They look cool."

"They do," she says.

"Like starfruit?"

Patti actually smiles. Chelsea approves.

But boys, to Patti, are easy to figure.

The girls can prove more challenging.

Sara the Red hooked up with Lucas in grade nine and they've been together ever since. Her friend Brianna got her claws into Steve in grade ten. So a day after the encounter in the library Patti was up in the Tech Booth, awaiting Chelsea. They had the tech for the final assembly to set up, and the auditorium below was slowly invaded by Spirit Squad, cheerleaders, ready to run routines on the stage. She caught her name, Sara and Brianna chattering, directly beneath.

"She and Lucas know each other from the enrichment thingy. You know she's crazy smart."

"Everyone knows," Brianna said. "So, what? She's gonna use her vast intellect to hit on our guys?

Good luck with that." She started a leap as she made her way towards the stage and let it became a lurch, trailing off into a hobble.

"Brianna!"

"Hey, I'll give to the charity. I just don't wanna have to look at her."

"You should feel sorry for her, Bri."

Patti sank back into the chair, kept the booth lights off. She can dismiss Brianna, beneath contempt. Late at night, it was Sara's words she recalled, and, hating her weakness, Patti wept.

The brothers haven't asked yet about why she "walks funny."

In the parking garage, teams of whiz kids signal they're ready.

Someone passes around forms asking viewers to sign away the right to sue. Doubtful it's binding here, but a nervous crowd goes along. It's part of the fun, like agreeing you won't sue over your heart failure before you walk through a Haunted House. Robotics, weapons, no one over twenty-five: what could possibly go wrong?

A heavy-set, brown-skinned man in black steps forward under unreal light. "Behind the orange pylons, we have The Extraordinary Legion of Über-Pwners with... *Legion!*" The wedge-shaped bot has a serious buzz-saw on the wide end and that modified flamethrower mounted on the narrow. It exhales fire, about two feet in front. Then it rotates. The crowd tenses up and applauds.

"And behind the gold pylons, the Altrusians, with... *Grumpy!*" Grumpy snaps and reopens his animal-trap upper-jaw against his cow-catcher front and waves and rattles his metal-snake tail. It has a nozzle on the end, though for what sinister purpose the spectators can only guess, surely not another flame thrower. The tank on Grumpy's back is sizable. The applause grows a little louder now; Patti and Chelsea turn to each other and laugh, just a bit. The Altrusians with Grumpy! What a kick.

Handlers hit switches and the bots begin to circle each other. People nervously deke away from nozzle-ends. Grumpy charges, tries to flip Legion with its cowcatcher jaw; Legion retreats and comes back with its buzzer. Sparks fly as it makes a dent. Two of the three Extraordinary Legionnaires cheer. *Yes!* Grumpy circles, tries a flip and a chomp; Legion spins and the flames shoot out, most likely lighter fluid or alcohol or propane. And Patti's right, it looks great, but it would take a good deal of focused blast or tremendous luck to fry a wire or critical circuit under all that metal, and these things just keep moving, awkward dance of metal on concrete. Legion gets off its final flame; Grumpy raises rattling tail and sprays a concentrated burst of water. The metal snake thrashes about in the steam and sprays more on the crowd than its opponent. It seems like mere cosmetics, a dominance display, but in the fog and confusion Grumpy spins and runs alongside Legion, finally flipping the fire-breather on its side.

"And the winner is... Grumpy and the Altrusians!"

People applaud. Mark yells out a guttural Klingon cheer. *MajQa'!* The four Altrusians jump and hug and pump fist. Chelsea is trying to wring out her top, which is running with water. She's taken the brunt of the loose spray. Her hair is soaked. Droplets spot her purple lenses.

Thomas seizes the moment and his purchase, a nanosecond before the idea occurs to his Klingon brother with the Vulcan robe. "You can borrow my *Empire* tee-shirt," says he.

16

Lady Susan Vernon
The Constellation Inn
Friday Evening

Mrs. Augusta Slesak adjusted herself in her chair, and swallowed more of her Moon Shot. She had nearly emptied her tumbler, and I predicted correctly she would order at least one more. She looked over at her husband. Her face seemed altogether wondrous, with her brown eyes and well-defined features. She looked askance at Miss Moon.

"It all sounds very trivial," Miss Moon had said. I felt a bit shocked, for her usually-pleasant voice contained a tincture of venom. We observed a moment of silence. The singer began a song written by Mr. Jimmy Webb.

Mr. Telfryn Tyde said, "I wanted to tell you where I was going today. I just figured nothing I could say would make a difference." Her face did not reveal the contents of her mind. "I said something," he explained to the group. "This morning. I may have phrased it awkwardly."

"He does this," said Mrs. Slesak, with an air of assurance.

"Wait," inquired Mr. Slesak. "Where was this?"

We counted another awkward moment before Mr. Tyde said, "She's from Sarnia, too." They at last and forthrightly explained how they had met through the church that counted her among its parishioners. Mr. Tyde, in spite of his free-thinking views, had assisted in a charitable enterprise there.

"We're in a Restoration comedy, then," observed Mr. Brian Slesak. He smiled, but only slightly, at his own wit.

"What is one more era?" inquired I.

"I don't think you're trivial in a bad way. I mean, the Janeites. No more so than the SF fans. The *fen*."

"Fair enough. And fair enough. We spent a half an hour earlier this evening discussing whether or not Jane Austen would have ever eaten cantaloupe."

"And?" asked Mrs. Slesak.

Miss Moon shrugged. "It was known in England since the 1700s, so possibly."

"They were growing it in Spain," said Mr. Tyde, "but her cantaloupe would have been the European variety. What we call cantaloupe the rest of the world calls *muskmelon*. It's like football not being soccer here. I hope everyone stayed awake through that."

"No. I'll have to share that with the Society. I'm

surprised no one mentioned it." Her eyes seemed to sparkle where another woman's might have been inclined to glaze over. I wondered if I could draw his attention, perhaps by asking if Miss Austen had ever enjoyed starfruit.

Miss Denise Moon was sitting on Mr. Tyde's other side, and I maintained an air of amusement and disinterest, as I pondered how my advice earlier that evening had so soon put her in my way!

The conversation continued for some time, before Mr. Slesak suggested we continue back in their hotel room. Mr. Tyde further recommended we get there by way of the "Party Floor." It seems the same level housing the consuite was demarked as the place where one might hold revels into the smaller hours. Miss Moon suggested herself too tired to stay up late, but agreed to walk the route before returning to her room. I regarded her announcement as good news indeed, though I noted her proximity to Mr. Tyde along the way. I stayed to his other side. While I doubted I had exhausted his store of fruit-related trivia, I wondered if perhaps other conversational pleasantries might shew us both in the best light.

The first party we passed proved but sparsely attended. They said they were expecting a larger crowd and a more festive environment on Saturday night. I was forced to contemplate whether they planned to begin the party anew the next evening, or if, indeed, the gala was to be continuous. Their offerings of food recalled the consuite, though they had a small bar operating under a convenient subterfuge. They served drinks free of charge, but displayed with considerable prominence a tin for donations. We stayed a short time. Miss Moon remained as well, discussing her church with Mr. Tyde. She seemed less inclined to convert him than to assure him they did many fine works. I would have relieved him of that tedium but Mr. and Mrs. Slesak spoke to me, with some affection, on sundry other matters.

We wandered the halls, passing once again the extraordinary, four-legged creature I had first encountered in the elevator. Mr. Slesak acknowledged he had no idea whence it came, though he and his wife both celebrated the detailed work that made it look so much a singular living entity.

The second party contained a larger crowd, and included a writer of some note in attendance at the conference. We again encountered the Triffids, who were relating a story of the panel they had attended earlier that evening. One of them had asked a question of a leading nature and a budding wit in the assemblage accused him of being a plant. People laughed or groaned appreciatively, depending on their particular natures. It was then that I found myself separated from the rest of our party, and in a corner with Mrs. Slesak.

"Do you find him attractive?" she asked.

"Telfryn? He has an appealing roguish quality."

"What about Brian?"

"Do you speak of your husband?" I felt slightly shocked, in spite of myself, but I smiled.

"I used to be the jealous type," said the audacious Mrs. Slesak, "but I have changed over the years." She then looked at me somewhat intently and asked, "If I may ask… Are you poly?"

At that very moment one of the Triffids returned from the bar, a fresh drink in foligial hand, human face visible beneath greenery like a child playing hide-and-go-seek. "Are you looking for Paulie?" said the Triffid. "Paulie should be back in the consuite."

The discomfited Mrs. Slesak made some apology for the misunderstanding, and the leaf-bearing individual continued on its way.

"Polyamorous," she said. She began to clarify what she intended by that word, when we became aware of a new presence. Miss Moon had sought us out, apparently intending to wish us a fond good-night. Her visage bore a look both disturbed and distressed.

Miss Moon pretended she had not heard so very much of Mrs. Slesak's curious discourse, but she soon thereafter excused herself. I acknowledge myself a bit shocked by the revelations and by the offer that might have been implied by her words, but I also correctly realized that Miss Moon would be excusing herself very soon, and unlikely to join the rest of us in the Slesaks' room. She looked somewhat sourly at Mr. Telfryn Tyde when they next passed; her feelings were waning. That he recognized the sudden paling in her sentiments towards him was clear from his face, though he had no means of discerning the reason. I felt, to be sure, sympathy for him, and not a little sympathy for her as well; Denise Moon was, in her own way, a likable innocent. Nevertheless, her discomfort worked itself perforce into my plans.

She coldly gave her regards and departed to our room. I decided I would at least drink with the Slesaks in their room. Indeed, my curiosity prevented me from doing otherwise.

17
The Former Gaming Party

Kirt's mother attends the church where I met Denise Moon on that Friday morning. Kirt worked for years as IT at a graphic design place, and has apparently taken on a volunteer position, helping with the church website. I last ran into my old gaming buddy two years ago, and he offered to buy me a beer. We sat on heavy wooden chairs in a pub with walls covered in framed images with no theme I could discern. He joked about the church, comparing the parishioners to LARPers and cosplayers.

"You want to see a photo," I said. I borrowed his cell and found the online image of me at a con, shaking hands with a stunning Stargirl.

He stared at it. "Yeah," he said, with a trace of disgust. "She *really* reads *Justice Society*."

I shrugged. "She *might*." I was surprised at his bitterness, because he'd been a gamer and a techie when I knew him, but not a comic book guy. For both of us the four-colour world was something we left in childhood. But I have affection for those heroes, and I marvel as they soar and sling web and hammer above mainstream crowds on the movie screens.

"It's bizarre," Kirt said. "Not even I touched comics in high school. Now twenty-three-year-old hipsters know the Guardians of the Galaxy."

"Heresy," I said. I was smiling less at my joke than the thought of Augusta, whose body I'd touched and whose secrets I knew. She, too, had loved a superhero, and, in keeping with the tenor of those times, had kept the affair clandestine.

Lynda Carter flashed across the TV screen as *Wonder Woman* when we were tykes and Augusta watched the after-school reruns. So while she was never a comic book girl she read Wonder Woman and has studied the Amazing Amazon, can retell her World War II origins, and how she sprang from the head of a polyamorous psychiatrist with a bondage fetish. Augusta knows her later incarnations, fighting in the dark shadows of the Crypt-Keeper and the sinister Dr. Wertham and then returning to the light with the Justice League and kookie sidekick Snapper Carr. In the seventies she made bold on the cover of Ms Magazine. George Pérez recreated her in the 1980s, which is the version I most recall. I'm sure Augusta keeps up with her twenty-first century incarnations.

And hanging at the back of Augusta's closet you will find a silk Wonder Woman bathrobe.

In high school, when Augusta set her mark and ran, she was the wing-breasted, goddess-blessed Amazon Princess, speeding for justice and womanhood. But her teammates did not know, for she kept these things in her heart.

18
The Augur of Lambton County

The Augur of Quaoar rests on a circular base approximately nine metres across, topped by three gradations, each slightly smaller, and then a tube sweeping upwards like the trunk of a tree, twelve metres in height, to additional circular shapes atop which contain most of the visible instrumentation. Superficially it resembles a nautical capstan. From its place on distant Quaoar it sweeps our system, hearing and seeing, and also merging with the thoughts and perceptions of select organisms.

Even now, we have implants that can read brain activity and do a fair job at translating these into speech. The Uirtkauwea have a significant technological lead in this area.

The closer the brain structure is to theirs, the more they can translate the neural patterns. Initially, the

Uirtkauwean Augurs learned a great deal about the thoughts of cephalopods, which principally concern spatial context, navigation, and food, though the waving and swirling that accompanies reproductive transfer also comes frequently to their minds. But our world has not been colonized and reshaped by cephalopods, so the Augur must continually adapt, allowing the avatars of its scientist-designers to infiltrate and learn from the very different brains of human beings.

Over a year after it commenced operation, the Quaoar Augur opened new eyes on a medium-sized Canadian city. The brain it found belonged to a juvenile human male. He looked upon deciduous trees and thought despair and broken things and feared the loss forever of emotions connected to nurturance, health, and reproductive success. Through me, the Uirtkauwea began to learn of human beings.

19

Lady Susan Vernon
The Constellation Inn
Friday Night

I had not previously encountered the word *polyamorous*, though I suppose, after a fashion, it might apply to my character. Lady Susan was, after a fashion, Georgian era poly. I myself have an arrangement with a gentleman who spends much of his summer in the Kawarthas lake country, at a cottage near Crowe's Landing, and thus near my home in Lakefield. He long ago took a wife, and our relationship remains but a summer dalliance, though one that has persisted over several years. We do not consider that these encounters, always occurring between June and September, prevent us from seeking other partners, though I acknowledge I have but little opportunity to do so.

What Mrs. Slesak appeared to be proposing was, indeed, a wickedness that even my namesake had not known. Mine hosts assured me that, among the fannish folk, one found greater acceptance of a range of lifestyle choices, and of the infinite diversity of infinite combinations. Nevertheless the Slesaks had, as a rule, remained quiet about such matters in their life, wishing to avoid any hint of scandal that might reach their various communities. This I understood. They have two daughters who, I am told, are of so unblemished and temperate character that Mr. Slesak claims he would not be surprised if they one day pledged a sorority, provided it held a reputation for conspicuous moderation. As for my reputation, I divined that Miss Moon's shy nature, combined with her uncertainty regarding the strange intelligence she had gleaned, would be unlikely to discuss her speculation about the Slesaks in the presence of others. Would not that set tongues wagging among the Janeites!

The four of us sat in their beige room, three of us drinking toasts of bourbon whiskey from paper cups. Mr. Telfryn took only water, and I wondered about his apparent desire to avoid the sweet dissipation that might be brought on by slightly immoderate consumption of strong drink. Mrs. Slesak, having excused herself on some complaint regarding the sweaty clothing she had worn since that morning, disappeared behind the sliding door of either their washroom or closet, and returned wearing a silk robe patterned to recall the costume of a noted Amazonian figure from popular fiction. Naturally assuming that Mr. Tyde knew about the Slesaks' unusual pastimes, I felt entirely too free to continue the whispered conversation she had earlier commenced with me.

"I admit to some trepidation. What, precisely, are you and your husband proposing?"

Mr. Telfryn Tyde looked about, his countenance displaying the most entertaining curiosity.

"I apologize if I misunderstood or misspoke…"

"I don't know that you misunderstood, *exactly*," said Mrs. Slesak, rubbing the tip of her tongue on the edge of her front teeth.

Her husband said, as much to Mr. Tyde as myself. "We sometimes like to have a little fun at the cons. If we find willing people."

Mr. Tyde's face had now fallen, with an overall effect of shock and bewilderment.

"Oh, Telfryn, dear. I thought you picked it up at some point. We're not as straightlaced as we look."

"We kept things from you, of course. When we first… At the time, Telf, you were still having *episodes*."

"We grew into it, gradually. As I said, at one time, I was rather the jealous sort. People change. I think most people need to kill the bull about relationships." She turned her gaze to me. "And Brian finds *you* very attractive."

I felt a blush come to my cheeks.

"He's not wrong."

"So again," I inquired. "Might I ask as to the

precise nature of your proposal?"

"We have partners outside our relationship, by mutual consent. We don't attend Roman orgies."

"Does Sarnia see many of those?" I inquired. I expected laughter and, indeed, her husband began to snort. The expression on her visage transformed quickly, as she focused on Mr. Telfryn Tyde.

I grant myself more than a little unable to read his reaction on his countenance on receiving this strange intelligence. I had at first thought him merely scandalized as, indeed, many would be. I came here thinking an affair might be an enjoyable diversion; the Slesaks' openness, however, does not sit comfortably with me. I also contemplated those specific details of their proposal of which I remained unaware. As I myself am unknown to the kinds of intimacies with mine own sex that I thought *might* be under consideration, it occurred to me that, even more so, that prospect might prove daunting to Mr. Tyde. Perhaps, too, his status as their friend of many years made such a change in the nature of their interaction beyond serious contemplation. I still found his reaction not altogether expected; he had the patina of one experienced in the world, and aware of its wickedness, even if he himself had not partaken. Whatever the cause, his eyes had widened and, it must be said, appeared almost to increase in circumference.

Then our hostess said, "Don't act so shocked, Telfie. It's not as though it would be the first time."

This was a most delicious turn of events. He looked over at Mrs. Slesak. "I never spoke about that," he finally croaked.

Mr. Slesak sipped his whiskey and swallowed. "Telf, she told me about *that* years ago. It just felt, I don't know, awkward, so I never mentioned it."

"Stumbo's funeral?" asked Mr. Tyde. A genuine alarm could be heard in his utterance.

Here the Slesaks appeared puzzled. "Was there another time, hon?" asked Mr. Slesak, of his wife. He sounded, to be sure, slightly appalled, though far less than another man might have been under similar circumstances. Augusta Slesak shook her head, and I believed her quite as confounded as her husband.

"Azogo," Telfryn said, pointing to the shadows in the corner of their room where, in truth, I momentarily thought I saw something moving.

"Telfie?" asked a most concerned Mrs. Slesak.

He dropped his paper cup and removed himself from the room.

20
And What Do We Do About the Crazy Naked Man?

Thomas takes his shirt back. Chelsea tells Kate, "I got wet!"

"What?"

"At a robot battle thingy!"

"The Yoshimites," says Mark, apparently thinking this will clarify matters.

"One of the robots sprayed water, and he had like bought this shirt, so…"

"Is everything okay?" Thomas asks, smiling. He has a half-moment of wondering if this new girl might be available if Chelsea falls through, but he sees daggers forming in Kate's eyes and it's painfully obvious she could kick his ass back to Holland, MI and not break sweat.

"We were at a robot battle," says Patti. "She got sprayed." Kate's desire to come here—that raised her in Patti's esteem. But if she cannot handle the con, after all, will she ever truly make Chelsea happy?

"This place is just a little... overwhelming."

Down the hall the crazy naked man lies beneath the duvet telling himself he will not be mad. I have maintained my sanity for years, and I tell Azogo of Uirtkauwea'ki, who sits on four folded legs, munching on my pretzels, that I will not be mad. It calls with expressive feline eyes.

"Do you not realize I am in you?"

My room seems larger than before. The floor glows star-white. A sudden freeze shocks and engulfs me. I wrap myself in sheets and duvet and drive the chill away; what I feel is the cold that is the child of Quaoar.

"Kate, this is Thomas and Mark. Thomas lent me his tee-shirt because I got, like, totally sprayed by a water-cannon last night..."

"At a robot battle?"

"Yeah..."

"Of course there was a robot battle."

"With a water-cannon."

"Hi, Thomas and Mark," says the Doctor.

"This is Kate. From our home town... and that's, like, the Doctor."

Patti finishes her mac and cheese, looks at the others and says, "Kate's Chelsea's girlfriend."

Chelsea smiles and Kate gives Patti a raised

eyebrow before decisively putting an arm around Chelsea, who leans her head on a shoulder. The Doctor bites her lip, but she's smiling. Thomas takes a moment or two to resettle his face.

"Oh," says Mark.

"I'll catch you guys later," says the Doctor, taking the bowl from Patti and dematerializing into her room, dodging Thomas's gaze.

Thomas takes a breath and then looks to Patti. She may not be Chelsea, but the movement aside, he thinks, she's really cute, in her own way. She likely hasn't had a boyfriend, he thinks, which would make the first the best she's dated. She knows a lot about cool stuff; that seems obvious. And the hipster nerd glasses are kind of hot. Sure, the style is *everywhere* now, but she *really* rocks them.

"I'll text my aunt about touring later. Or Sunday. What the hell?" They follow her eyes to the man emerging from a room down the hall, dishevelled and quite naked. "You have got be kidding!" says Kate, as she considers the body standing down the hall, liver-spotted and beginning to wrinkle, paunch and penis hanging down, sagging ass reflected in the mirror above the half-table at the corridor's end.

"Telfryn?" Patti sees my eyes and recognizes they're not mine.

And I look behind them and repeat, "Azogo!"

Kate casts a side-glance at Chelsea. "Is this that LARPing thing?"

Patti braces herself against the wall.

Thomas asks if they should call hotel security. But the girls say, *no*. Whatever my issue is, Chelsea assures him, I'm a good man, an old fan, and something must have gone awry. They don't want to create a problem.

Mark says, "He could be on meds."

"If he's not..." says Thomas.

"That's totally not LARPing."

Patti asks about my friends. What is their name? It sounds like *Sleestak*.

"Uh, at least maybe you guys should get him back to his room."

"The Slesaks," she says. "Yes." She looks at the brothers. "Get him to his room..."

"Are *you* okay?"

"Into the room." She nearly falls over, and Chelsea supports her. "We will find the Slesaks. He came with them. They can deal with him."

Awkwardly the brothers, who, it must be said, have no previous experience directing paunchy naked middle-aged men, take my arms and guide me back to my bed.

They're teens, youth, and I wish I could be their Wise Old Man, but instead I'd likely play the grizzled gatekeeper, the Crazy Old Guy who warns the teens they'll be doomed if they continue. Azogo lifts a hand and puts one of its three fingers to its slitlike mouth. Then Azogo winks. I wonder why an alien would have recognizable expressions. Did it learn the *shh!* gesture from human contacts, from me, or is it a natural one among creatures with vocal mouths?

"Why is he asking about alien gestures?"

I try to keep the story clear in my head, but the Uirtkauwean interface scrambles nearby thoughts and I do not always know which ones belong to me. The younger brother has developed a fondness for Patti but, in light of their initial meeting and his own unsuccessful past with women, he has no idea how to communicate the fact. Thomas just wants a woman, any woman. He met a female engineering student last year, on a pub crawl. Jasmine, like the tea or Augusta's hair. He regaled Mark with the tale, with a *yeah, hot enough, but not, you know, porn star hot. Hot amateur hot, with braces.* They haven't had *sex* sex yet, but it loomed as a possibility, before the year ended and she went back to her small town in Indiana for the summer and they communicated by appchat. She thinks he's cute, and just needs him to listen now, to talk with her. Kate and Chelsea swam off the shores of their town. The Uirtkauwea sometimes engage in a whirling behavior which may or may not be equivalent to human dancing. During this ritual some groups place strips of multicoloured fabric on their arms. The fabric sparkles as they spin, shimmering beneath the Uirtkauwean sun.

Someone wanted me, years ago. I didn't see it. My fondest recollection of a woman isn't even sex. I want to tell them about Augusta and the Dog Star and how life will keep moving and you have to make decisions and other serious matters. My brain rests in the room and the past and in their lives, the lives before me, and in some alternate timeline where, perhaps, lemonseed grows in that old *Star Trek* Ferengi mug on the windowsill, but it's my picture beside Augusta and, I suppose, a very different pair of children. I'd still work in Chemical Valley, I suppose, in that other world.

Is Azogo a muse from the heavens or does it lead me onto the frozen deserts of Quaoar to tempt me? I see what may be the surface of Uirtkauwea'ki, great blue oceans and tree-tall growths resembling outsized leaf-bearing gourds.

The boys hesitate, and then step from the room. Now what?

Mark once again asks about Patti, who sits on the floor. "Are you gonna be okay? I mean, your legs?"

"My brain." He looks puzzled, but she's long got this one. "Cerebral palsy. The problem's with the software, not the hardware," she explains. "Sometimes strong emotions"—he does not realize how hard it is for her to admit to such a thing—"affect my movement."

"Sometimes her legs just stop working," Chelsea says.

Chelsea helps her to her feet, as she has for most of their lives. Patti grimaces when she sees Kate on the other side, an arm that would require no assistance to raise her up.

"So."

"I realize this is like, weird," says Chelsea.

"I have no idea what weird is here."

"This is weird," says Mark.

"Chels," Patti says. "You know the Slesaks? From last night?"

"Jetsons and zombies and the CN Tower." She looks to Katie, who doesn't want to know. "We could find them."

"I'll stay here with the guys," Patti says. "In case. Maybe…"

"Be right back," says Mark, and he rushes towards the stairwell door.

Chelsea looks over at Katie, but the taller girl says, "We'll find his friends. Maybe I'll even get to one of those panels today." She takes out her cell again, to text some version of an update to her aunt. She omits the part about the schizophreniform naked man.

"Ooh!" Chelsea says. "We've missed the start of the *Doctor Who* one."

"I imagine you've had enough of the Doctor."

"We'll ask around the consuite. And we can get breakfast." They walk down towards the elevator, Kate realizing she's now mired with the fen. "There's one later today on contemporary folklore creatures. We might, like, miss the computer panel, but we'll be done by the time they're talking about folklore. You won't, like, need to have read or watched anything to understand that."

Patti watches them.

They're holding hands.

21
Lady Susan Vernon
The Constellation Inn
Late Friday Night

No more than she would have approved of recent pastiches that pair her characters with zombies and Victor Frankenstein, would Jane have approved of how we handled what mine hosts termed, "the three-body problem." But I acknowledge myself no stranger to scandal.

I grew up in a small town, though one which saw tourists in summer and private school students come autumn. We're connected to Canadian literary history. A set of sisters very different from the Bennets, Susanna Moodie and Catharine Parr Traill traipsed through these bushes and stricklands, cleared trees and roasted bear. Their lives felt like too much work, noble and conducive to strong character though they may have been. I was a reader, a borderline scholar, though never among the top rank of our school. I wanted too much to enjoy myself. Girls regaled the school with stories of meeting the rich and elite students who attended the private school or the celebrities and others of means who held estate-like cottages on the nearby Kawarthas, future heroes, legislators, fools, and villains. These girls I knew and I found a place as the quiet one of their group. We made a few parties held by people whose wealth or notoriety placed them well out of our range. They were a gateway, as I saw it, to the sort of soundtrack-scored adventures teens were supposed to have. Some of my friends dreamed of meeting a Mr. Darcy, though I doubt they would have known him by that name, any more than I would have.

The summer subsequent to tenth grade we found ourselves at a party held by a wealthy boy who attended the private school and whose family owned one of the estate-like summer homes on Stony Lake. Their children converged while the parents were out of country. The elder sister arrived with friends from Western University, while the boy we knew had an assortment of guests from two schools, private and public. Even the younger brother attended with a couple of other fourteen-year-olds. The rooms were lofty and handsome, and their furnishings suited to the fortune of its proprietors. It exceeded anything we would have considered a cottage on the lake. A Japanese painting of a lakeside scene adorned the wall behind the couch.

Amenities were set by the water. They chiefly

consisted of Adirondack chairs, paper plates, red plastic cups, and a karaoke machine. This was then still an exotic novelty, something we might have heard people did in Japan. Party-goers explored the lake with canoe and a paddle-boat. In the evening, to the questionable delight of the shoreline, we turned on the machine and sang an assortment of selections from the musical *Grease* and the popular songs of the day. Drunk enough to be bold, I joined another girl in an inebriated version of "Shiny Happy People." I fancied a boy named Adam, and clearly, I had caught his eye as well. He returned with a remarkable rendition of "Misty." I was not alone in finding it touching; we're certain we heard applause from down the shore. Over the course of the subsequent hour, I found myself alone with my young gentleman on a couch in one of the smaller rooms. I resisted his most urgent requests but, after our dalliance had nevertheless progressed to a considerable degree, I agreed to give him a blow job.

Little more might be said even without the restraints of propriety. He agreed to call, but I suspected he wouldn't. He sought only a five-minute dalliance, and was the sort, I know now, to think me fortunate I had received as much attention.

The girl who had chauffeured us to the party had, indeed, consumed more than would recommend her for performing the same service on the occasion of our departure. We nevertheless made the return drive with her. On Northeys Bay Road not far from the highway our happy progress was impeded when her car made acquaintance with a large tree. We had been driving slowly down the deciduously-shaded roads, so no one came to serious harm. The girl driving threw fits of vexation, before we formulated a plan to make our way home by some other means, and report the car (which belonged to her father) stolen from the party. We knew we would have to acknowledge the party, the lesser of two evils. Alas, as we fell upon the details of this deception, we became aware of the flickering lights of a vehicle bearing the distinct markings of the provincial police.

As a consequence of this misadventure I found myself secluded from the world for the foreseeable future. I acknowledge, however, that after the initial anguish had passed, I began to fare a little better at school. My parents were right or, so it seemed at the time. This wasn't me. I drifted from the group. The following year, I read *Pride and Prejudice*.

The other girls grew and married and remade themselves as well, into people whose lives some might not readily reconcile with events that had happened when we were, by the broadest definition, maidens. Only at twenty-one did I rediscover Jane. I understood her then, and fell in love. As time went on, I drifted from those old friends, and spent more time with books. I only slightly recognize the earlier edition of myself. That said, I fall regularly into wickedness, but in accordance with a schedule.

The Slesaks represented for me a new concept, a

couple faithful in their infidelity. Having consumed an adequate amount of strong drink and, having passed over the course of the evening through gradations of increasing affection, I planned to persevere. They were moved, however, by the abrupt departure of Mr. Telfryn Tyde from their room, and the mood had passed. We remained up much of the night and attempted to contact Telfryn Tyde. When that failed, they agreed to check his room again in the morning. I was disconcerted and uncertain of where I was in the hotel and I gave my regards before returning to my room for a sleepless night. It removes something of the excitement of a liaison when one has the permission of the wronged party. I did not know if I wanted to see them again, for this dalliance is a tawdry and sordid one.

In the end, perhaps I am just a simple woman from the lake country.

22
The Robe

"We *should* leave him rest," says Mark. He sounds apprehensive but there's an uncertainty in his voice. "But we, we might not be able to stop him if he gets up again. And it's, it'll be easy to put him in a Vulcan robe."

Patti assents. But Thomas finally asks, "How is he our problem, exactly?"

"We know him from cons," Patti says. "I think he has some... health issues. It's only until his friends get here."

"You're not all traumatized from seeing a naked man? Well, that's a relief."

"I'm not always the most understanding person. But I think we should try here."

I open my eyes. If I could take a mallet to a wormhole, build a time-machine, I could stop invading extraterrestrials, serial killers, and corrupt politics and well-wishers. Are the Slesaks *Sleestaks*, the icky reptilian raiders from *The Land of the Lost* with scales for flesh and hooks for hands? I had bequeathed to Augusta the place of honour, the place of all and any woman I would ever meet, and hid my treasonous acts from my friend and saviour, Brian the Sarnian. Brian the Saurian? They rebuked me. I slept with Augusta and kept silent for years and none of it mattered. I might as well have been a wedding gift to his wife.

I start to sit up.

"The robe," says the girl.

Michael Rennie played Peter, I think. "No," I say aloud. I'm imagining Michael Rennie as Mr. Carpenter, arriving in an interplanetary craft with a message of hope. "But then they turned dark. Things from another world." The youth anoint me and array me in a robe as bright as a flash of lightning. I am returned from the desert and shall go forth. Azogo of Uirtkauwea'ki walks with me and in me.

"Jesus, he's...!" says Mark.

"Hold him!"

I see the Slesaks shedding dried skins, rubbing and peeling, throwing the calcium-rich remnants on the barbecue as an appetizer before dinner, father and mother and charming 2.5 daughters all technicolour smiles and 1953 coiffures, lemonade and sprouts chlorophyll green in the Ferengi mug in the window, dark doings at night-time. What transpires behind closed doors? On vacation? Do the daughters hand over the late-night caller to Augusta or Brian, retreat to the slumber party and say, with casual disregard, '*it's one of Mommy and Daddy's fuck-buddies*?' before playing another round of *Mario Kart* and putting sleepyhead's bra in the freezer? As the night draws colour from suburban Avalon, do darker things make their way into the grey lands? But by now I cannot separate reality from dream from conjecture from mental invasion. My brain reorganizes itself into alien patterns, and I feel the racial fear of the Uirtkauwea, who eons ago shared their planet with predatory creatures like great insectoid reptiles who fed upon them.

Patti's wishing the adults would get their asses here or at least reconsidering whether they would have fared better with able Kate as my keeper. I'm stronger than I look. Azogo is stronger still, and if Azogo is with me, who can stand against me? I swing my fists and the brothers retreat. Clad in my robe I bolt for the elevator lobby.

23
Denise Loses Hope

As old as Cain and Abel, or Heungbu and Nolbu. Denise went through a period of admiring her sister. She still admired her sister. But the jealousy was old now, and the judgments so much a part of her life she cannot remember a time when she didn't feel inferior, coveting what belonged to the older, perfect Hope Moon. She remembers them driving with her parents and their cousin Hyun to the Shrove Tuesday Pancake Lunch at the church. She was squished in the middle in the back seat of the Hyundai Stellar and the prickliness of her good winter coat pressed into the skin of her arms. They drove up the hill and to their church. A newer building, as churches go, it looked like several pale-bricked houses arranged together by a giant child. Her father unlocked the trunk and she and her sister got their sheet music, sealed in plastic, and her violin, safe in its case.

There were rows of tables and the floor of the

church hall was dotted and damp with melted ice and snow. Their church served the traditional pancakes but also *kimchijeon*, which the non-Korean parishioners tried cautiously but praised effusively.

A special treat for the pre-Lenten revelry: several of the young folk would perform musically. The minister introduced each in turn: Jung Cho, Timothy Deck, Cheryl Maddox, Hope and Denise Moon.

Jung played a flawless Schubert *Menuetto* on flute with impossible grace, tiny prodigy with too-large instrument. Denise could not even see him from her seated position, over the people in front of her. Timothy performed passably a truncated "Ode to Joy," hidden behind the piano. Cheryl had a false start, but afterwards, acquitted herself admirably in the singing of "The Pancake Song" while the church organist accompanied her on piano. The Moon sisters concluded with a duet, a simplified arrangement of the *andante* from Haydn's "Surprise Symphony." Hope played the piano; Denise played her violin.

Number 94 gets its nickname from the sudden *fortissimo* chord at the end of a quiet second movement of the opening, the classical music equivalent of a pie in the face.

The room opened up before her, faces she saw each Sunday in church but seen from the front, what the minister must see. In the critical second movement she fell out, hit the surprise, the critical moment, a beat too early, off the piano. *Surprise,* indeed. She felt blood rush to her face and the violin squeaked. Her sister continued and she found the place and played perfectly to the end.

The audience applauded.

When they were back at the table her sister glared, just once, and then did not look at her again.

After pancakes she asked to use the washroom. On the way back, her eyes still swollen, she entered the small room used for Sunday School. She sat and read illustrated Bible stories, opening onto other worlds and times, brunet Adam and blonde Eve, modesty preserved by the convenient growth of trees of all kinds. An angel delivered to Mary the news of her pregnancy and the Devil, tanned and horned, tempted Jesus in the wilderness. Eden, Egypt, the Holy Land: these places were far more interesting than anywhere she had been.

A year later she still wanted to begin afresh, and her parents finally agreed to let her switch to cello with Mrs. Park. Denise felt secure behind the larger instrument.

Her sister worked hard; Denise worked harder to accomplish less, felt herself in her sister's reflected light. Her parents held out Hope to her, Hope the Exceptional. Hope the students' council member. Hope the scholarship winner. Hope the high school music teacher. Hope the doctor's wife.

They remain in London, Ontario where they attend that same pale-brick church and raise their children. Hope maintains thriftiness even when she goes shopping; a local, high-end boutique has a basement filled with fine fashions, unsold, slightly out of date. Her sister walks down those steps, sometimes alone, sometimes with their mother or her close friends, and purchases high fashion at discounted prices.

Hope's regime of exercise and dieting ensures she never has a pear-shaped butt.

Denise found a job in Sarnia with the library and sings in her church choir. Otherwise, she tends to play her music for herself. She sees her parents far less often than either they or her sister considers appropriate—"Only an hour away!" Her parents have long since stopped trying to introduce her to single men. She wants the attention until she actually gets it; she has trouble liking any man who would want her. But Denise's nieces and nephew love her. They will likely grow up to be more successful than she is.

Denise Moon reads. She occasionally tells herself stories about the characters as she reshelves books in the library, and sets aside the patrons' holds. Sometimes she writes these down. And she recalls the day when she was a senior in high school, the hormonal incoherence and inelegant drama of the halls overwhelming, and she first started reading *Emma*.

She kept a diary around then. After Jane, she didn't have crushes and hobbies. Denise had *fancies*.

They're learning how to tie cravats, now, while they wait for the Regency dance lessons to begin.

They have high tea to look forward to and the general meeting, of course, though by then, she will be preparing. Afternoon will end with an Anglican Evensong (from the 1662 Book of Common Prayer, but it will also include the orison "Another Day Now Gone," penned by Jane herself) followed by dinner. She's tried to enjoy the morning, and has chosen not to ponder too deeply the scandalous activities of Miss Mistie Matthews aka Lady Susan Vernon. And she wishes she had never met Telfryn Joncourt Tyde and his degenerate associates.

24

<del>Lady Susan Vernon</del>
Mistie Matthews
The Constellation Inn
Saturday Morning

It is a disconcerting circumstance to observe more legs than one anticipates for a given circumstance. I meditate, in turns, on the hooded figure and the wanton couple. All of the costume's limbs seemingly all functional: a most peculiar and ingenious design it must be! I try to raise my encounter in the elevator as a point of interest with my room-mate. Alas, I am afraid Miss Denise Moon has quite done with me, and offers only the coolest of pleasantries. At breakfast I imagined the eyes of the Janeites gazing at me as my classmates did, all those years ago, the September following my youthful fall from grace. Of course, they had neither knowledge nor an actual scandal, as yet, and in reality were pleasant enough, and all aflutter about the Regency dance lessons and the Evensong later in the day. In Miss Moon's eyes alone did I stand accused of impropriety, though, as she herself conformed to etiquette, her accusations she held in silence.

When instruction began in the proper tying of cravats, I declined. I am, in fact, an old hand at such matters.

Thus did the latter half of Saturday morning see me resume my visit with the Slesaks in their beige hotel room. I felt as awkward and as lively as I had in that imposing cottage—whose owners from former times, I learned, some years ago, fell into difficulties, and were forced to sell the property that had been the setting for my youthful debauch.

"Do you comprehend the oddness of the circumstances for me?"

"And yet," said Brian. "Here you are."

"Here I am." I spoke of my perennial gentleman, and our alliance of convenience.

"Does his wife know?"

"Ah. I don't know. But she isn't *present*. What would the teenage Augusta say?"

"The teenage me would be shocked, but..." She waved her hand. When we ladies removed our clothes, we could not help but assess each other, compare one to another. I acknowledge Augusta has kept in better condition than I have. I can draw no conclusion about the price exacted by either of our lives.

Circumstances required we pay *some* attention to each other. His hands found their way into the necessary places; hers took actions less needful. Once we set about the conventional business of love-making, I fell to Brian, who has some gifts as a lover. He's remarkably well-endowed—perhaps too much for his stabbing approach. I suspect Augusta likes it aggressive. Once he had discharged himself, she spooned his body as he did mine. Only much later did conversation resume, and, after Augusta and I in turns returned from the washroom and repositioned on our backs, the discourse alighted, after a time, on the problem of Mr. Telfryn Tyde.

"What did he mean by that, some other time? He mentioned a funeral."

"Yes. Greg. Gregory Stumbo, friend of his who was murdered."

I moved the tips of my fingers to my mouth.

"He was there when it happened."

"Oh."

"It happened outside a dive back home. He was in his wild man phase, then. Telfryn was. But there was nothing between us then. I was pregnant at the time, for Christ's sake."

"Wild man. He still wears a bit of that," I said. "Certainly, enough that he stands out in *this* group."

"We're a lot more diverse than people think. You're drawn to him though? The 'roguish quality'?"

"At first," I acknowledged. "But…"

"He appears to be tidally locked," Augusta said, prompting a braying laugh from Brian.

"He watched a friend die. What an extraordinary thing."

"We figured," said Brian, "if he didn't have an incident after that, he was never going to have one again."

"His—I think they tentatively call it a schizophreniform disorder. A spectrum kind of thing, I think. They think. But yeah. I drove him to Stumbo's funeral." She stopped awhile in thought, and we both knew not to inquire as to what her eyes were seeing. "I was worried for him, but he was fine. He's been fine since. We've always worried about him, Brian and me. I don't know why he mentioned Stumbo's funeral. Hon, I would've told you if there'd been another time."

Brian's look suggested serious but detached contemplation, a doctor discussing a patient. "Maybe it would have been good for him," he said. They joined hands, just like lovers.

Later, Augusta and I quietly discussed literature while Brian slept. This naked and Amazonian woman handed me two novels, Robert Charles Wilson's *Spin* (autographed) and Emily St. John Mandel's *Station Eleven*. She described them as accessible literary SF, good places to start. "So much out there," she said. "I can make a list, Asimov to *Z is for Zachariah*. These are loaners. I hope to see you again. I'm pretty sure my husband does, as well." She smiled.

They seem to hold genuine affection for each other. Augusta used the word *compersion* to describe their feelings in such situations, when seeing their beloved in bliss with another. I wonder how often she truly experiences the feeling, but I did not query her further on the matter. The wife of my longest relationship does not or chooses not to know. I don't imagine she would ever be terribly *comperse*. I take pleasure in these times, but they evoke no strong feelings. I wonder if love exists, or if people simply agree to share a common delusion, of one sort or another.

I looked at the clock and realized I had missed the start of dance lessons. Though I had wanted to attend, I recognized that I might bathe and take my meal at leisure, and thereafter prepare myself for Evensong and the events afterwards. Circumstances perforce hastened my plan; there was a knock on the door.

25
Geneses

Kate walks with Chelsea down the hall towards the Slesaks' door and recalls a prelapsarian time. The summer before grade nine, they went to the shore, the main beach spread beneath infinite blue skies, down from a lighthouse that now serves as a museum and modest tourist draw, and they played volleyball in the water without a net, skin exposed by swimwear, eyes wide like cubs and kittens. Then they had chicken fights, these kids she'd known since kindergarten, Sara on Lucas's broadening shoulders, and Bri atop tall Randy Roberts, and Steve, to much laughter, on *hers*. They splashed into perfect small waves and then drank bottled water on the beach. The Lake Huron waves grew higher with their spirits, raising up swimmers on the swelling surf, knocking down waders to buoyant screams, cresting to white at shore.

Sara and Lucas have since moved from shoulderjousts to pelvic thrusts. Roberts still hangs with them, but he has grown an ugly edge, drinks to puking and treats females on the fringe of their social group like interchangeable holes. Steve is dating Brianna and her judgment Kate fears the most: Bri whose strange news and pharisaic pronouncements could uplift or cast down the obscure girls.

In private, Bri tells Kate she made the right decision to stay away from boys for now. She assumes it's because she works so hard, plays so hard. "You're like the girl version of Lucas. Anyway, hon, once you turn that sex thing on, there's no turning it off."

She thinks of the beach again as she waits at the door. She and Chelsea recently spent that consummate afternoon, two girls on sand and surf and neurochemical bliss. They stepped onto the beach near two boys doing bottle-flips by the trash can, trying to get it to land upright. They walked past and turned also from the silos and industrial docks down the way. Lake Huron glimmered aquamarine at shore, turned turquoise and teal and sapphiric where it curved into horizon. The girls ran into the waves hand in hand (girls can run hand in hand) and dove and played like children. They touched the bottom of the lake—further from shore, Chelsea said, than she'd done before.

Chelsea had brought a transparent tube containing sparkles and stars: a portable, private galaxy. They floated on that until the waves grew too choppy, and then they brought it ashore, and dried out siren-stretched on rocks near the white-stone pillar of the decommissioned lighthouse.

"I saw those two kids on the shore. They were like still bottle-flipping."

"Whatever floats your boat, I guess."

"Maybe it was a new bottle. Like, they just returned to bottle flipping?"

Kate asked about Chelsea's family, and about what Patti was doing. Chelsea asked about the Rose Point Challenge. "The guys are already getting ready for next season. Well, football. Boys' basketball isn't till later. You know, we're all gonna be senior team now."

"You were *already* senior team."

"Oh, and they got so gross. I mean, after the game. Steve was talking about this one time, last year, when the seniors and juniors had those back-to-back games? I guess on the buses back, they had... They mixed them up, senior and junior, you know, all the offense on one bus and all the defense, instead of senior and junior buses? And the senior guys were naming girls and raising hands if they slept with them or did stuff with them."

"That's disgusting."

"I guess Roberts raised his hand for *Maddy Hills*." She shook her head. "A third of them are BS'ing, I'm sure."

"Did the coaches say anything?"

"Probably not. I don't know. Sometimes I hate we live in a world where guys act like that and… people think bottle-flipping is cool."

"Especially the bottle flipping."

"Yeah. So annoying."

A kid with lamb-shorn hair clambered by on the rocks and then climbed from sight.

"Katie?"

"Yeah?"

"*You* live in that world. I like this one."

Toes touched. Chelsea peered through purple spectacles, but Kate—Katie—saw the eyes beneath the glass and felt like she should blush.

The evening ended with a kiss.

She knows she can never return.

Augusta Slesak, clad in a *Wonder Woman* bathrobe, peers from behind a partially open door. She recognizes Chelsea, but she's surprised and suspicious.

"Telfryn Tyde," says the teen. Augusta steps into the hall as they tell the tale.

Chelsea receives a text.

They soon find their way to my room, where Patti sits with the boys, and Mark notes that the con is certainly proving particularly memorable. He glances over at the half-eaten bowl of pretzels I set out Friday afternoon, but refrains from taking any.

"We just don't want him to get in any trouble," says Augusta. "He's had a difficult life. And…" She reiterates what she knows, in broad strokes. That I once had episodes. That I have not had any in years.

"We're sorry."

"He's not your responsibility."

"Yes," says Brian. "Thank you. You tried. You know, enjoy the con, kids. We'll look for him."

"At least you got him dressed."

"Right. We'll get you your robe back."

But Patti says, "Can we have your cell numbers? I mean, if we see him, we can text."

They agree to her request, and the Slesaks say they also will inform the young people if they find him first, a courtesy. Kate invites Chelsea to brunch in the hotel restaurant. Thomas and Mark and Patti take the elevator to the party floor, where Mark helps her into her seat at the consuite. The boys go for drinks and bowls of vegetarian chili on rice. Patti declines food; she has eaten already.

"It was caffeinated?" Mark asks.

"No question." They're sharing now. She talks about how they know Telfryn, and their history at the con. Her father has always booked the room, and, in the past, turned up to keep the matter legal, working part of the day from the room and leaving them be at night. "He's a physicist. He pretty much just works. He's sort of a noted physicist. Well, noted Canadian physicist." He's let the girls stay alone this year. He has few dealings with that brilliant female student from long-ago, but this is his daughter. His favour rests with her. "I'd tell you his name but then you'd have no idea who he is. To quote Chelsea, *we don't put physicists on hockey cards.*"

"They'd be physicist cards," says Mark, scoping the web with his cell.

"A valid point," she says. "His last name's not Washington."

Thomas asks, "Yeah… Chelsea and Kate…?"

"It's about time." She gestures to Mark, who hands over his cell. Patti searches up her father's name online. "She and Chels have been playing *maybe* for the last three months. Well, Kate has. She struggles with saying *lesbian* out loud."

"It might lead to things," says Mark.

"Like what? An orgasm?" She hands back the cell. Mark reads a little, eyes growing a little wider. He shows it to his brother.

"Your dad's a big deal," he says. "My God, he's got a Wikipedia entry."

I recall learning his identity, a con or so ago. *Where were you, asks the great I Am, when I laid the cosmic foundations? Who marked off its dimensions? On what were its footings set, or who laid its cornerstone while the morning stars sang together and all the angels shouted for joy?* Patti's father would have nodded his head and handed over a diagram scrabbled on the back of a take-out receipt.

"Undeniably. He's also kind of a dick." She takes a sip of reconstituted juice. "I'm still going to see him tomorrow."

"That's good. I think that's good."

"You want his autograph?"

"Wait, I'll see, I'll see if I can find his physicist card for him to sign."

They laugh, and even Thomas can see the light. Chili consumed, he excuses himself and makes his way to a panel, saying, as he leaves, "I'll report any encounters with Subject Jaybird." Mark turns again to Patti.

"No guy back home? Oh—you're not, you know, like your friends? If that's not..." His brother, he knows, would be facepalming about now. *You dord.*

"No. And no boyfriend, either, Mark."

"No?"

"There's this one guy... I think he's funny. He's kinda hot. But he's got a girlfriend."

"You're probably too good for him."

"In some ways, you're right." She looks into his eyes. "But I can be difficult to get to know, so, you know."

"Really? You? 'There's a planet where what you said makes sense?'"

"That was a snid rude."

"*Lilbit.* You wonder why this guy at school isn't interested. I would've, I mean, I would've avoided you. Out of fear."

"A wise man. Why didn't you?"

"You were, you know, I... Then we were at the robot competition. The robot battle. We have a robotics team at my school, my old school, but we didn't have many girls."

"So you just want me for my robotic skills." She

starts to rise, and he extends a hand—which, after a moment's hesitation, she takes. "Just like every other guy."

"Well... you probably just want me for my chemistry skills."

"You got me. Chemistry's a science I haven't really developed my skill set in. I'll need a good chemical engineer if I'm going to take over the world."

He's touching her hand, uncertainly, but she doesn't pull away. "Okay. I'm officially applying to be First Chemical Engineer in the Patti Washington Regime."

"I'll give your application the most serious consideration."

26

An Avatar of the Uirtkauwea Ponders the Role of Wingless Octopodes in Ritual Human Conflict on Ice

We're in a small storage room available to the cleaning staff. The off-white walls have been scuffed. Cleaning supplies stock the shelves, in industrial-sized tubs and jugs. The door requires a key. I have no idea how I am here. I have just enough space to sit against the wall. An extraterrestrial or, strictly speaking, the image of its avatar rests in front of me, looking at me with compassionate though terrifyingly large eyes.

I think of Kate on the beach and Patti in the tech booth, at once powerful and vulnerable. What, Kate wonders, do her peers conclude when they see her with Chelsea? Mistie Matthews retains an alluring quality, Denise Moon I find fascinating, but Augusta Slesak and I bear the traces of a chemical bond.

I look over at Azogo, who has guided me to this place.

"You were among the first *Homo sapiens* whose brain the Augur on Quaoar could successfully read. Human subject #3. Male. Juvenile."

Azogo sounds particularly excited when saying "male" or "female," as the Uirtkauwea do not conceptualize separate sexes and lack altogether the social equivalent of gender. One hears the quotation marks in his voice, or whatever passes for quotation marks on Uirtkauwea'ki.

"One set of issues when you're interfacing with an octopus propelling itself in the deep of ocean. Or even a confused octopus, thrown onto an ice rink in a Red Wings hockey tournament. We have found this, by the way, to be most puzzling. Why does a group of ritual warriors named for avian wings have a cephalopod as a symbolic avatar? And why do people offer them as ritual sacrifice?"

"I never really followed hockey," I tell it. "My dad might have known." I feel a humming in my head.

"But another matter with a species possessing your sentient complexity. Like us and not like us, as we have come to say on Uirtkauwea'ki."

"The con must *really* be confusing."

Azogo pauses before replying. "The people participating in the rituals here do not believe in their literal truth. That resembles much of the thinking on Uirtkauwea'ki." I again have visions of those whirling dances. "The somewhat younger 'females' who find you reproductively desirable will be attending the simulation of a religious ritual today. Might we go?"

It stretches upward, arising like an alien craft on its four legs. I put my hand on the floor to get up. Azogo reaches out an arm.

I take it.

27
Mistie Matthews
The Constellation Inn
Saturday Noon

I rejoined my compatriots for the General Meeting. Miss Denise Moon, I knew, would be practising the musical score for Evensong. Indeed, we had at an earlier time arranged for me to take notes for her, as she alone represented her chapter at these proceedings! I fulfilled faithfully, if not enthusiastically my duty to her. Afterwards, I received again compliments on my attire, which I have mended, on the whole, adequately. I nonetheless longed by that point to dispense with Lady Susan Vernon and acknowledged that she would not be present at Evensong. The woman dressed as a Regency widow expressed concern and disappointment, but I assured her *I* would not fail to miss the occasion, though I would be in a different guise.

"I so look forward to that," she said. She began to

elaborate on the Regency dance lessons. I tolerated her descriptive ardour for as long as etiquette required, before excusing myself, using the pretense that I must change my costume. I nevertheless, as I strolled towards my room, took a circuitous route which found me in the gaming room of the SF folk.

A pleasant, portly gentleman welcomed me at the door, and requested I fill out a ticket for the next draw, which, he assured me, would occur within moments. I glanced across the tables of folk playing, as I believe, the Gothic pastime called "Dungeons and Dragons," and sundry other unusual amusements, certainly unknown on Box Hill. Miniature dragons laid waste to a tabletop Tokyo. Ships took imaginary flights to the stars in simulated conflict. Devil Bunny, apparently, had need of a Ham. Beverage cans stood empty like Redcoats in rows. A flush of recognition swept me as I sighted some of the youth to whom I had been introduced the previous evening: Thomas, Chelsea, and a maiden named Kate, whose voice I was certain I recognized from Mrs. Slesak's cryptic encounter at the doorway that very morning. Young Thomas was in the midst of expatiating on a man and woman attending the gaming room, who provided on behalf of a manufacturer complimentary libations that promised enhanced energy. He noted that the man's outfit, while suggestive of a well-known heroic figure, bore a chest-insignia associated with the libation's manufacturer. The woman dressed in a manner that suggested the naval-derived uniform worn by some female pupils in the Japans. Young Thomas christened the pair *Captain Buzz Ener-G* and *Sailor Kepler 153-b*, but he nevertheless took a beverage from this smiling young woman.

"Have you seen Telfryn?" asked young Miss Chelsea. When I answered in the negative, they noted only that he was unwell, and that his friends, the Slesaks—I must, they assured me, recollect them from the night before—should be notified at once. "They're all concerned about him."

"He'll be dressed in a Vulcan ceremonial robe."

"We hope."

The Slesaks indeed had alerted me that morning that a matter of some importance required their attention, but failed to explain to me that it might connect to the strange behavior of Mr. Tyde on the previous evening.

"If you see him… Do you have the Slesaks' number?"

"I do indeed."

"These people are really into games," quoth young Kate, looking around the room with the unmistakable air of incredulity. Charming Chelsea returned the emotion. It seems whims and inconsistencies do divert her.

She laughed and then squeezed the taller girl's bicep. "That's some serious jock privilege, Katie."

"Those games are diff…" But Kate recognized she should best leave that thought incomplete.

"If you provided catheters, some of them would

never get up," offered Thomas. "Are you guys doing the parties?"

"Oh, like, well... There's this one panel on modern monsters. Like, present-day folklore. We might go. And then there's this evening panel on, like, fandom and alternate lifestyles later tonight."

I explained that I have already attended far too many events for which I have not paid the expected price, and that, in any case, I would be expected at the Evensong shortly.

"You didn't pay for the con?" asked a surprised Thomas.

"I'm here for the Jane Austen event. We're a smaller group in the same hotel. Did you not know?"

"Oh. I wondered why there were so many historical cosplayers."

"You do have awesome costumes," said Chelsea. "I think that's worth the price of a few events."

The girls next asked Thomas about the alternative lifestyle panel—the general topic of which, I must quietly reflect, included me.

"I'd feel out of place," said Thomas. "I suppose I do have an alternative lifestyle this weekend."

"Oh?"

"Involuntary celibacy," he said. Kate rolled her eyes.

Oh, but he is an attractive young man, in his own way, a gentleman just finished his first year at the university.

He then of a sudden said, "You know... There's a

Jane Austen one. A board game! I saw it earlier." I was understandably intrigued, and he led us to the place on the sales shelf where was found the box containing *Brides and Prejudices: A Game of Miss Jane Austen's England.*

"How does one win?"

He perused the text inscribed upon the box. "*Making a good match.* Apparently, by landing a wealthy husband."

"Typical," said Kate, in a disdainful tone. Chelsea giggled. The girls excused themselves, reminding us of the promise to send word by text if any encountered Mr. Telfryn Tyde.

"Intriguing," said I. I had a sense that Miss Moon might enjoy such a pastime. Surprises—I recalled Miss Austen's words—are foolish things. *The pleasure is not enhanced, and the inconvenience is often considerable.* Yet I felt deeply that, though I owe Miss Moon no accounting of my private business, I should somehow make amends between us, and it might best be a surprise, the origins of which she would induce.

He replaced the box upon the shelf where it had sat.

It was at that very moment that the portly gentleman attending the door heeded those gathered in the room to take note. He drew from the helmet of no militia known to me, and read the string of numbers that designated the winning ticket.

I smiled, the sweetest smile of the afternoon.

28
Azogo the Great Attends an Anglican LARP

O gracious light, pure brightness of the ever living
Father
In heaven, O Jesus Christ, holy and blessed!

*Now as we come to the setting of the sun, and our
eyes behold the vesper light, we sing your praises, O
God;*

Father, Son, and Holy Spirit.

*You are worthy at all times to be praised by happy
voices,*

*O Son of God, O Giver of life, and to be glorified
through all the worlds.*

Someone brought an antique stained-glass window
of St. Helena and hung it with great care behind the
makeshift altar. It lends a spiritual gravitas to the
recreation. The Janeites assemble, some in the more
ostentatious fashions of their era. The priest in his

vestments and artful locks looks every bit the country parson from the early nineteenth century. He is in fact, a contractor and former choirboy from Burlington, who plays the role because he enjoys the music.

The small crowd has gathered in the room, an oasis from the rest of the inn, with its bustling travellers and cosplaying fen. The singers, members of various church choirs, perform for the crowd or sing with them, as occasion warrants. When the singers do not perform a cappella, two women accompany them. The older, silver-haired woman, dressed as a Regency widow, plays an electric keyboard set to organ or harpsichord, as the music requires. Denise Moon plucks and strikes and bows the cello.

On a dais two doors down, panellists run through slides and discuss histories, from folklore to fiction, the Devil of New Jersey, the Monster of Nith River, the Goat-man of Pope Lick. Rare—but not unheard of—is the crypto-beast that propels its way, like the giant squid, into legitimate zoology. Others lumber into lore from uncertain sightings and unfocused filmstock. They're stoked at campfires—some cropping up before, and others after, their spooky stories circulate. A few have their reputation inflated from hoaxes straight out of *Scooby Doo and the Curse of Silver Lake*. The Internet, once a slender player in this game, has, as in all things, taken the lead.

Some remain mysteries. Any rational explanation seems weaker than the feeling that the thing just exists. The human brain is a marvellous organ.

Kate and Chelsea struggle to pay attention. But they've experienced a few feelings of their own for which the rational explanation falters. They have each imagined aspects of a story, twice told it to themselves. The thing exists. Try to stop a chemical reaction in process.

They sat close and have moved closer. Fingers grapple with fingers. *There are such beings in the world—perhaps one in a thousand—as the creature you and I should think perfection; where grace and spirit are united to worth... equal to the heart and understanding.*

Soon any glance they exchange excludes the room, the scholars, the fen, and any other imaginary phenomenon.

They quietly leave and walk hurriedly past the Evensong.

The Janeites and others recognize that a newcomer has arrived at the door. Some wonder if it's lost, looking for the SF costume competition. It walks on four legs; its huge, soulful eyes examine the room. Instead of turning, it sits at the back, on the floor, its hoodlike robe settling like a skirt, and it appears to focus on the sounds of string and key. Denise tries not to see it. It's affecting the mood, ruining her concentration, creating in her head more stir than that unexpected foul surprise all those years earlier on Shrove Tuesday.

She will address the distractions later. She has learned through years of Mrs. Park's lessons, Kiwanis Festivals, church recitals to focus on the music, give herself over to the music. She will play that music for the audience, whomever they may be.

O Lord make clean our hearts within us.

Back in her room, on a bed redolent of salt and human scents, Chelsea moves closer to Katie and they meet eyes like sweaty-palmed youth in an iPhone film.

"Everyone else our age, like, sneaks around, right?"

"Yeah. Sara's mom got her on the pill but then she and Lucas are still expected to sneak around."

"We could totally be everyone else." Mouths interface; hands and tongues initialize. Katie moves atop Chelsea with assurance neither questions.

Elsewhere on the floor Thomas, strangely elated by his decision regarding the prize game, passes his own room once more and confirms the presence of a purple twist-tie on the doorknob. Good for his brother. As for Thomas, he has arranged a rendezvous later that evening.

Downstairs the Janeites take a minute to recognize the second late arrival. Her costume has changed from the devilish red dress of the previous night to a grey-blue ensemble and a churchworthy hat. Most recognize the outfit as one she wore two years previously as Catherine Morland. She looks weary and dissipated, but perhaps wiser. Evidently, this is Miss Morland at *Northanger Abbey*'s end.

She sets an anachronistic tote bag beneath her seat.

The day thou gavest, Lord is ended,
The darkness fall at thy behest;
To thee our morning hymns ascended,
Thy praise shall sanctify our rest.

Patti and Mark sit on the edge of a hotel bed, white cotton sheets surrounded by beige walls.

"I've never really had a girlfriend. Which is... I mean, the girls I know seem to sort of like me. I was in band, you know, and pretty much everyone's really friendly. I just... I don't really know how to talk to girls if it's, like, if, you know, if it's about going out with a girl. I just think they won't be interested."

"But *I* would? What, I don't count because I walk funny?"

"No. No! Not at all. See, we're both here, so we're both fans. *Fen.* And you're into tech and other cool stuff... So, you know. I mean, why me?"

"You're going to be the chemical engineer among my minions, so there's that. You're cute, so you might as well do double duty."

They kiss. Patti melts a bit, reflects on how good this feels. Even the slightly alien sensation of his tongue in her mouth grows acceptable.

O Lord, open thou our lips.
And our mouth shall shew forth thy praise.
O God, make speed to save us.

O Lord, make haste to help us.

Denise Moon watches as the crowd relaxes. She looks up, but Mistie Matthews will not meet her gaze. Instead, Denise turns her head to the alien visitor. The large eyes seem soulful and moved. It blinks twice.

She recalls the Bible verse. It would have to be John: *Other sheep I have, which are not of this fold.* And she persists in playing. She will not miss a beat of time. The congregation follows the ancient rites.

Them also I must bring, and they shall hear my voice; and there shall be one fold, and one shepherd.

With awkwardness in her movement, Patti reclines on the bed, the top sheet of which has folded provocatively back. Mark strokes her pixie-cropped hair and kisses her cheek and then her ear. In a gesture that cannot avoid feeling clichéd, he removes her glasses and places them on the bedside table. She smiles. She's imagined such caresses many times.

"You can still see?"

"I can see you."

He lies beside her and they continue kissing. Hands engage in cautious exploration. He steels his resolve and climbs atop her, and takes a knee to his groin.

"Are you okay?" she asks. She tries unsuccessfully to suppress laughter.

"Jeez, Patti, if you didn't, if you didn't want…"

"Mark… Sometimes that leg doesn't move when I

want it to."

"Oh. Right." He pauses and after a moment he looks more composed, though the knee to hard-on doesn't feel any more pleasant. But he recalls their earlier conversation. Strong emotion does this to her.

Despite his discomfort, he smiles. *All right, then.*

She focuses for a moment: *okay, you need to move.* She used to talk and later, as she grew older, *think* to her dysfunctional leg—though she knows it's not the leg that's the problem. She doesn't want to look ridiculous though, and part of her suddenly finds this needful thing ridiculous. Instead, she talks to Mark. "Okay. You might have to move that leg into position manually."

"So it's okay? For me to move it?"

"Well, as long as I'm on my back, Mark."

His eyes grow brighter.

"You have a condom or something?"

"Patti?"

"Hey, I wasn't planning on this."

Mark nods. He stumbles across the room and finds them in the drawer near Thomas's bed.

Denise Moon bows the song to its conclusion. Azogo reaches out like God on the Sistine ceiling. She could swear the eyes are real. Denise wipes a tear from her cheek.

The grace of our Lord Jesus Christ, and the Love of God,

And the Fellowship of the Holy Ghost, be with us all

evermore. Amen.

Someone's sweat runs between her breasts. A universe pulses, and they rest, share private thoughts, wash and rinse, return to the bed, drift awhile in and out of sleep. As the Janeites leave their makeshift pews, Katie says, "Ask Patti to thank her dad for arranging your room."

"So noted."

Waves pass. Katie props herself up on one elbow. "We didn't really talk about that panel."

"I had my mouth full quite a bit. Yeah. Oh! We totally have to ask the guys about Michigan Dogman. Mark and Thomas. Remember? They're from Michigan. Maybe they've heard of it."

"Uh… Uh… Right. The one the disc jockey made up for April Fools? And now people say they see it." She strokes and moves Chelsea's hair behind her ear.

"Maybe they do. I think we should get a local monster, like, back at the Point? That would be shiny. Ooh! Or a local alien."

"*He* just made it up."

"He just did. And now, it's like, real. I mean."

"'Real.'" Kate makes the quotation mark with one hand.

"It has a Wikipedia entry."

"Well then."

Chels stares intently into Katie's steel-blue eyes. "We need to make *us* real," she says.

In the makeshift chapel, the contractor priest approaches Azogo and it rises up and adjusts the hood. "Thank you for coming to our service," he says. Azogo blinks and the mouth moves, a rubbery expression like a puppet's smile. Cautiously, Denise Moon and Mistie Matthews approach the alien. They each reach out and it takes each hand with one of its own, much to the amusement of the LARPing Christians. The contractor priest shrugs his old shoulders, and he and two others take down and pack up the stained-glass window, rolling thick blankets around.

O Lord make clean our hearts within us.

Lady Susan (Catherine Morland? Or just Mistie Matthews of Lakefield, Ontario?) says, "I shall explain, if you'll listen." But first she turns to the alien. "Are you well?"

It nods, but does not speak.

She reaches into the top of her dress and beneath her bodice, and retrieves her iPhone.

Patti, stripped, splayed, thinks of the crude vernacular, *getting nailed.* The veil has not been torn before. There is blood, but not much. Sweat, which they wipe from each other's brows. She rests near him. He seems blissful. She's not unhappy. It is done.

29
Mistie Matthews
The Constellation Inn
Saturday Night

I explained in whispered confidences as best I might the developments with Mr. Telfryn Tyde. "You must know," I told Miss Moon, "that he departed last night very early." Mr. Tyde said nothing as we ascended the stairs and guided him to his room where the Slesaks, alerted by my text, awaited without.

"Nice robe, old friend," uttered Mr. Slesak. He had been the keeper of Mr. Tyde's extra key, and took the essential measure of unlocking his door.

"I am not mad," said Telfryn.

Mrs. Slesak addressed us quietly and with a calm demeanor. As Telfryn Tyde slept, the couple acquainted us with some details of his history, without going too far beyond what decorum and his privacy might permit. "It's very odd," she remarked. "He's had no real incidents in years."

"We figured he was past it."

"I'm not a doctor, but it seems odd."

Miss Moon excused herself to use the washroom. I recollected my gift in the tote bag and placed it on his table, with the tag indicating her name.

When she returned, he again awoke to a familiar face. "Denise Moon," he said.

They spoke awhile, and, in response to his questions, she discussed the Evensong and the intricacies of the music, and endeavoured to explain "drawing out the sound" to someone with no musical background.

"I didn't know you played cello."

"It seems there's much we don't know about each other, Mr. Telfryn Tyde."

Some brief and hasty conversation led to Mrs. Slesak directing her husband and myself out of the room, with assurances granted to Miss Moon we would remain in the hall, and return at a moment's notice. I took my tote bag and we retired to the hall.

"Thank you for sitting with me," we heard him say.

We left the door ajar, and Augusta and I sat as though adolescents against the walls opposite the door of Mr. Tyde's room. She produced her cell and reread my text: **Have found Tyde & will bring him directly. Seems himself though cried when she played cello.**

"We didn't want to drag you into, well, anything else. You're not responsible for him. And yet… Here we are.”

“We do appear to be together again.”

“I could go get coffee,” said Brian. We thought this a good use of his time, though we felt some concern about our ability to control Mr. Telfryn Tyde should he once more take leave of his good sense and nature. I discoursed upon my encounter with the youths, and my chance reunion with Mr. Telfryn Tyde at the Evensong devotions.

“She likes him,” whispered Augusta. “It’d do him good to feel that again.”

“Love exerting a medicinal influence?” I said, with perhaps some intimation of irony, though (I must insist), a willingness to believe that such a thing might be.

As we had become in the short passage of time since meeting rather more than strangers, it seemed no great intrusion into her privacy to ask further about her long history with Telfryn who, it was clear enough, must have been a man of considerable natural appeal in his youthful days.

“God, yeah,” said the most forthright Augusta Slesak. She paused a moment whilst two youthful girls paraded by, one wearing ears that suggested nothing more than a cat and hair dyed (I must assume) a most brilliant shade of cerise.

A trembling transpired in my breast. I reached for my cell phone. “You may have, as they say, eluded a bullet.”

“Maybe *he* did. He had some problems, I know.

He dealt with them. I found Brian. We started as friends and learned to love each other. It is kind of a con, but I'm happy."

I bit my lower lip, without force, wondering what the guileless Miss Moon might say about Mrs. Augusta Slesak's most remarkable sentiment. As Mr. Slesak returned with the coffee, I knew I must bade both of them farewell, for I had an innocent flirtation from earlier that day who required some small compensation.

30
Quaoar Station

"Yeah, I thought I was gonna get lucky with that cosplaying MILF," says Thomas. He's returned to his room late in the Witching Hour, spinning like a 50s flying saucer, mind heavy with intoxicants. His brother walked Patti back to her room, having remembered to remove the purple twist-tie while she was in the washroom. He washed only his hands. She does not let him in her room where Chelsea opens eyes and waves.

"She left... After..." Patti raises an eyebrow and Chelsea trills a giggle. "She's gone to her aunt's. I'll see her tomorrow."

Mark returns to his room where his drunk and stumbling brother talks of MILFs and a party. "The Yoshimites had a party!" His voice staggers, awkwardly, through his words. "They had a *Dalek* at the bar. You know, *Resistance is f...* No. Wait. *Exterminate!*" He laughed. "That blonde *Doctor Who* chick was dance with Grumpy I mean like, they were remote controlling. The robot. They were remote controlling the robot."

"Not her."

He raises an emphatic hand, one finger extended. "Not her. The robot. I think she's... Doctor Four now. Or some of the old-time Doctor Who. *New Hope* era Doctor. You know, had the long-ass scarf? We had this whole conversation about... Something. After dinner? I tried..."

"So about the MILF? I think she, she called herself Lady Susan."

"Oh... Yeah... See I let her have my... Her name's 'Mistie' though. Look at me! She was cosplaying... Lady Susan Morlock or some shit. I won a free game in a gaming room. Somehow Mistie convinced me I should donate it and she'd buy me dinner."

"Oh?"

"She agreed to buy me a late dinner in the Starlight."

"Sounds like a harrowing experience."

"*Fly me to the moon*... I lost a game. I could've had a free game. I don't know. She said it would help her out with someone. She could have just *bought* one. But yeah... Like it was better if we had some kind of complicated plot going. Yeah, so she won the game... Door prize. She won the game room door prize. But she didn't have a con badge. So she asked me to pick it up using mine. She left during the one party though." He raises himself from his bed—pausing a minute to stop the unsteadiness of the room—and then begins removing his sneakers. "Anyway, the Doctor chick wasn't interested. I don't know. I thought university... UM... I'd get all this pussy. I do everything I think but girls don't seem to like me. I feel like such a dord sometimes."

"You know, she's probably waiting, probably waiting around the faculty of engineering for you to ask her out."

"The Jane Austen MILF is *not* creeping around Ann Arbor."

"No, I mean, someone else. Some girl. I don't know. There was that one girl from Indiana in your class? She sounded promising."

"Yeah... Jasmine. I mean, she has braces and her town has a Turtle Fest."

"Don't disrespect the Turtle Fest. We have a freakin' Tulip Festival."

"*In the month of May people come from far away. And it's rililodiculous.*"

"*You* watch *The Clone Wars* cartoon."

"She seem nice and wait you watch it too sometimes. And it's a an *animated series*. Not a *cartoon*."

"See, Patti wouldn't care. Okay, she thought—she thought the Klingon outfit was dorky, but..."

"A woman of... taste. My brother has found. A woman of taste."

"I think that whole thing's right, you know. Someone wants you. Somewhere."

"Well, *you* got lucky."

"Exactly! King of the Purple Twist Tie. I think I've got myself a long-distance girlfriend."

"*Qapla!*"

"*'IwlIj jachjaj.*" *May your blood scream!*

The boys try to rest, knowing they'll be leaving—well, at this point, not in the morning, but certainly, before sundown on Sunday. Thomas's summer job has ended but Mark has another week scooping up frozen yogourt before they load up the Odyssey and hit the 96. They or I dream of a future colony on the edge of the solar system, a place on the Kuiper Belt—Quaoar, perhaps—a planetoid dwarfed by the vastness of space beyond, whence we might head out to the distant stars, isolated and full of promise.

I cross the grim garnet ground beneath trans-Neptunian skies. The pinpoint of the sun shines more brightly than the moon back home. Stars recede beyond counting. Even here, the Slesaks would find me, and tell me I belong on Earth. They will act as they act, not in accordance with my plots, but their own. The Slesaks will remain in my mind and would do so even if they did not remain in my life, as does Stumbo and Sonia and my mother and father.

Azogo departs from me, an Uirtkauwean avatar returning information to its Augur nestled on Quaoar, the ruby amphitheatre observing our system, shimmering also beneath the frozen oceans of Europa and behind the braincells of snails and cosplay preachers and science-fiction fen.

It has inadvertently brought me visions and wonders, but it has also rent me from within. When next we meet the Uirtkauwea, perhaps the encounter will be less clandestine.

Remember me to Uirtkauwea'ki.

I awake from that dark and frozen lake. Denise Moon, smiling, shows me *Brides and Prejudices: A Game of Miss Jane Austen's England.* "You didn't need to get me anything." I'm ready to protest, but even I could not fully account for my early wandering. What knowledge did she have? I settle into my confusion, and make a mental note to check my wallet or credit records at some future date.

"The Janeites'll be thrilled to see it. Thank you again, Telfryn. You're really very sweet."

"It was sweet of you to sit with me."

"Maybe we can play it together. When we're back in Sarnia."

"Of course!" I say. "It's been awhile since I played tabletop games. How do you win this one?"

She played upon a cello and drove away the dark thoughts I'd summoned. Under her pull I was restored to health and I, as a small token of my gratefulness, bought her a game. Neither notion seems far-fetched. Perhaps in a year or two, none would be able to gainsay either claim and be held credible.

31
Ascension

Early Sunday morning, Patti tells Chelsea, "It happened," matter-of-factly, while sitting on the edge of the bed. She shrugs. "He's not my boyfriend. But I think we both got what we were looking for."

"Maybe," says Chelsea. She imagines Mark was looking for a good deal more, hoping for a good deal more, but she does not say this. "But so?"

"So?"

"Uh, question of the day, Patti. What was it, like, *like*?"

She thinks a moment. "A bit sore. But it had its good points."

"Yeah?"

"A little bit. So, a little sore. But warm. There was this one incident with my leg."

Chelsea laughs. "I totally wondered if that would happen."

She describes that incident in further detail and

shrugs, as Chelsea struggles to stop giggling. "We got it working."

"You always do."

"I think I can like to be touched."

"Imagine."

"What about Kate?"

"Her legs are great."

"So you guys are... *You Guys?*"

She nods her head. "She was fucking *awesome!* I'm going with her and Aunt Izzy today."

"So we'll all be in town."

Chelsea completes hair and make-up, and then slides open the closet. "Who knows? Maybe we'll go to Semi next year."

"Well, it'd be a shame to miss the chance to wear a poofy dress and watch people have sex on the dance floor."

"I know, right?"

"Her friends... I mean, none of *ours* will care. But hers might be a little scary about this."

"I know," says Chelsea. "But I think she'll come through." She puts on the purple-lensed spectacles. "It wouldn't be fair of her to break my heart."

Patti smiles and hopes.

As regards Patti and Mark, I think Chelsea may be right. As I said, I encountered Mark a con later. She and he spoke for a time Sunday morning, before she departed. They also keep in touch, through a form of telepathy, the social networking and texting and appchatting which their generation thinks is normal human behaviour. I shudder to think what we'll do with Uirtkauwean tech. Patti moves easily on, it seems, but Mark will keep her forever in his heart, even until the end of his days. He recalls his final vision of her that August morning, merging with the light streaming through glass doors at the front of the hotel. She makes her way to her father's house, dines with the professor and, I would like to believe, extends a kind hand and an understanding she has not felt before, even if her first loyalties remain and must remain with that resourceful woman on the Point who in some other timeline might have been Dr. Washington. Kate and Chelsea tour campus like a couple of teenagers looking to the future. Gazing out across the green from King's College Circle, they see, framed by Baroque-revival Convocation Hall and the brutalist Medical Sciences Building and looming distant, the upward-pointing finger of the CN Tower.

I do not see any of the girls again that weekend. There will, of course, be other cons. They will come again.

32
Mistie Matthews
The Constellation Inn
Sunday Afternoon

It is a truth universally acknowledged that the Sunday of a weekend gathering must run at a slow rate. The weary family of Mundanes (for so the Speculative Fiction Folk have named those who do not share their interests) joined the check-out lounge, their child transfixed this time by the uniquely-coiffed Paulie, who was conferring with the hotel's employees regarding some unresolved matter regarding questionable use of the luggage carts.

As regards my precipitancy with the university student, I was inclined to set it aside. It is probably best he chose to parlay, however (I suspect) unproductively, among women closer to himself in age. I think in any case I should have spurned him. He recalled for me too much a certain cottage on Stony Lake.

I waited for other Janeites to join me for our Sunday breakfast, and found myself drawn to a station in the lobby, evidently established to provide the space-folk with a central hub for information. A young blonde woman occupied the chair, clad in a wine-coloured jacket of a style that might nearly have passed on a dashing Regency Buck. She carried an electronic device, the purpose of which I could not conjecture. I consulted with regards to membership for the coming year. "I'm here with the Jane Austen group," I explained. A man in a kilt passed by.

"Yours or ours?" asked the young woman.

It was then that I spied Mr. and Mrs. Slesak, Miss Denise Moon, and—wonders!—Mr. Telfryn Tyde, conversing, as it seemed to me, quite amiably. A few of the Janeites approached us, and I made such introductions as circumstance required.

"Will any of your extraterrestrial guests favour us with their presence today?" asked the widow.

"You'll find the alien population a bit diminished this morning," responded Brian Slesak.

"So no chance those plant-people I've encountered will join us?" I inquired.

"They're delicate costumes," said Telfryn Tyde. He sounded, to me, at least, perfectly within command of his senses.

"Leafier than in the book," added Brian.

"I imagine by now they need repair."

"Oh!" said Denise Moon, with a smile. "And I had such hopes for those shrubberies." We paused and stared. "What? It's from the 1940s *Pride and Prejudice* movie adaptation."

I smiled back.

"But of course!" said the old widow.

"A little *too* trivial, I guess," said Miss Moon.

Telfryn laughed enthusiastically.

33
The City of the End of Things

Denise Moon, her ticket cashed in, accepts a ride back to Sarnia with Augusta and Brian. We wait downstairs in front of the Constellation, amidst a small pile of luggage. I talk about how my father stayed with my mother, even when people would have understood his leaving. "They're both long dead," I explain.

"I'm sorry."

She tells me about her sister's success, and her tensions with her parents, and how her sister and mother buy excess amounts of remaindered designer clothes, only slightly out of fashion, at a store in London.

"What will they make of me?"

"Don't go there, Telfryn. It doesn't suit you. Anyway, I have a cousin in London with a white wife," she says.

"Scottish-English-Canadian. Both very successful and beautiful people. I've never heard my family speak against *her*."

"It's not *that*," I say. "Denise, you could walk into any coffee shop and find five more-promising gentleman friends. You could join one of those online sites. Isn't that what people do now? Online dating?"

"My family have introduced me to many promising gentlemen. I found you on my own. Look, don't think of us as dating. We're *not*. We're hanging out and I'm helping you get back into your life."

"So I'm the leper you want to feed and clothe? The traveller by the side of the road? I fell among robbers on the way to Jericho?"

"You fell among *something*."

A horn honks and the battered Honda Odyssey passes by. It's Mark who drives and waves at us. His brother rides shotgun, dark glasses on his head. "Great con," Mark shouts.

"Spread the word," I say, and then I turn back to Denise. "Moon and Tyde."

"An improbable fiction."

"I'll bet your Caucasian cousin-in-law is also a church-goer?"

"Of course." And, really, what do I know about the vastness of the cosmos? I understand faith in the *past*. But I find it passing strange this intelligent woman, not so very old, believes like the aged ladies the pastor loves believe, and an appeal to evidence and logic will be neither useful nor convincing. "I believe," she says, "a particular tradition has meaning. What is with your people? Everything is a debate. Then again, that's true of the Janeites. Telfryn, we had tears in our eyes at the end of the Evensong. Why does that happen, if it's not something genuine?"

I shrug. "Emotional connection. Brain chemistry. I've been known to get misty-eyed at Linus's speech in A *Charlie Brown Christmas*."

She laughs. "God, I watch that every year. I have the DVD but I usually end up watching it on TV. '*Fear not! For, behold, I bring you tidings of great joy, which shall be to all my people.*'"

And, I suppose, to mobile plants and hexapedal aliens from Uirtkauwea'ki.

She puts her head on my shoulder, something she has rarely, if ever done, to anyone else. And then we hug. For a moment I recall the pregnant Augusta on the sidewalk in December, and the passers-by who imagined us a couple. When I open my eyes I see a shift in Denise Moon, and a smile of great joy. She whispers, "I felt your heart leap."

I return the smile and, thinking on Azogo, I say nothing.

The Slesaks pull to the front of the hotel, still bearing signs of a con. We load the car and Brian takes us onto the highway and back into the world.

Troll Bridge

She took three years to learn to walk. Patti is a patient girl.

When Chelsea got her out to a basketball game to watch Kate play, helped her up into the stands, she observed movement her body would never manage, even in dreams. Kate outmanoeuvres, outplays, and out-and-out terrifies the girls on the other team. "Like perfect code," says Chelsea.

Kate wasn't Chelsea's first, but Brad Kwan was Tech Club and Cassandra Rose, something momentary, and Chelsea remained by Patti's side, assisting with stairways and rocky places. But now Chelsea's all about Katie, and Chelsea's vivacious nature allows her to pass breezily through that crowd—at least, much of the time. Plenty of older, kludged-together codes can bug up matters. Nice town, but if Patti swings her cane, odds are strong she'll strike redneck. She doesn't need the cane, really; she got along most of her life without one. She likes it though; it has a weathered look, a wizard look.

So maybe Chelsea has herself a *real* girlfriend this time; Patti will make time with her Magus.

She sits on her bed with one of the school's

notebooks, temporarily liberated, and logs into the wireless down the street, routes through a virtual private network, and signs into the site. *Magus* has posted three new images:

The photo of a charred soldier, face blackened, smile skeletal, captioned: *Improper or repeated exposure to ultraviolet radiation in this tanning bed may cause damage to skin.*

The second photo exposes four girls sharing a hot tub. One is less attractive than the others; maybe it's just the face she's making. The text: *Buy three and we'll throw in a fugly* ABSOLUTELY FREE!

The girl in the third photo might be fourteen. She stands a few feet back, her pants down, and her hands on her hips. The top of her crotch is in plain view: *She thinks only her boyfriend has seen this. Other posters call for* more!

Patti grimaces. She doubts it could be a selfie; the lens gazes down at the girl from *somewhere*, and she seems oblivious to it. Patti studies the image awhile, and wonders if there's more. A memory strikes her and she clicks around the site. She finds the photo Magus posted the week before to disgusted praise and mock arousal: an old woman in a grey washroom, her dress, a cultic robe sort of thing, raised, underpants around her ankles, wrinkled legs showing, hand reaching for paper.

She compares Smiling Crotch Girl with Drop-Drawer Lady. The girl obscures the background, but both shots look like they've been captured in the same locale. She's guessing a public washroom. Patti looks from the screen to the golden Lucky Cat on her dresser, bobbing its paw to rhythms she cannot hear—distant music, perhaps.

Tonight, Chelsea and Katie are hitting a party, where they will play just friends until they find a reason to leave. And Patti will ponder these latest developments online. She imagines her Magus's life in nights alone, posting from a room filled with empty cans and crumpled fast-food bags.

* * *

Kirt returns to St. LARP's on a Saturday night in October, when they hold their fundraiser on the stage in the rectory basement. Someone has tried to disguise the drabness with orange streamers and a harvest display, pumpkins and ears of multicolored corn. It's his yearly sacrifice, part of the give-and-take that keeps his ma smiling and inviting him over for Sunday dinners.

Aging women like his mother need hope, and she really believes his father lives on somewhere, his scruffy face and the sage smell of his aftershave, the extra helpings of home fries Sunday morning with frequent sprinklings of salt. Otherwise her church has few real beliefs, as far as he can tell. They're more like a live-action role-playing game, and so he has dubbed them St. LARP's, though not to his mother's face. Their events do, he admits, serve better food than the average gaming party.

They have a choir reputed to be the best in Lambton County, and a new minister who brought with him a flat screen and the ringmaster style of a big box church. Some of the other old fogies find the colour and noise disconcerting but, his ma insists, over Sunday dinner, this new minister *has* drawn a few more young people. Kirt cocks one eyebrow, asks her to go on.

"They had three girls go up, right in front of the altar. Lovely young girls. They did an upbeat sort of a song with gestures. Just at the age where we often lose them, you know. Now, the one girl's shorts were too short for my taste. For church, I mean. Maybe just doesn't realize she's gotten, you know, too old to dress that way."

Kirt smirks. He doubts that very much. He takes another slice of roast breast, and draws with his teeth and tongue the fat beneath the skin.

And so he accompanies her to the rectory basement in his dark brown mock-turtleneck and dark brown pants and, dragged from the back of his closet, the brown sports jacket she bought for him. Gray heads abound, peppered by a few young choir members and younger children. He looks to the kitchen; he knows they will have baked goods at intermission. He will simply have to deal with two interminable hours of what passes here for entertainment.

A young boy plays the violin. He plays it well, but it's still a violin. The M.C. rehashes a joke that must have been old when she was young, and then introduces the next performer, the youngest member of their choir.

"Oh," his ma whispers. "That was the girl who sang in the summer."

The girl wears a minidress, white with delicate blue flowers and leaves, like bone china. Beneath the dress, her young legs show implausible fishnet stockings.

She gives a studied, awkward introduction and then sings something from Mozart in crystal tones. Her voice sounds a little like whoever sang for Brit Ekland in *The Wicker Man*, de-aged several years. When she gestures with her hands at the end, her minidress raises, ever so slightly. Kirt shifts a little in his seat.

At intermission his ma patters about how lovely the first half has been. He grabs a marshmallow square with chocolate on top, and his eyes scan the crowd for the Mozart Girl. He catches sight of her teacup dress as she steps out into the hallway.

"I have to go to the washroom," he says to his ma. He licks melted chocolate from his thumb and index finger.

He heads down the dark hall, around the corner. Pipes run along the ceiling. The door to the women's washroom is closed. He steps into the men's, a single use affair with drab floors. She flushes, a few moments later, and he lets himself breathe awhile after she walks away.

Kirt stands alone in the hall. He quickly peeks into the grey room: mirror, sink, garbage, tampon dispenser. He looks at the vent, over the sink, directly across from the toilet. It has wide vertical slots.

* * *

Magus: Hai! Liking your captions, sweetiebytes! If your really a girl, nice to meet one with a sense of humor.

> **sweetiebytes**: I's a girl. With boobs and everything. Yeah, lots of girls are bitches who don't understand humour. Or computers.

> High school sucks. Hey, your some kinda bigsht here, aren't you?

Magus: You could say that. So what about a photo?

> **sweetiebytes**: I'm shy.

Magus: Shoot some of your cheerleaders.

> **sweetiebytes**: With a camera or a .22?

Magus: Kek. You have cheerleaders then?

> **sweetiebytes**: We have cheerleaders. Many of them are total bitches.

Magus: Colour me shocked. Don't suppose you'd sneak a camera into the changeroom for an old guy? For teh lulz?

> **sweetiebytes**: LOL. Anyway, funny site.

Magus: Thx. Welcome aboard! Ever find any of the

pics hot?

> **sweetiebytes**: No. I don't know. You take some of these?

Magus: If they're going to make it so easy, they have to expect to get captured.

> **sweetiebytes**: True dat.

* * *

H, E, Double L, O! That's the way we spell hello HELLO! From up above to down below we say hello!

"More lights," radioed Brad Kwan. "Try five and six."

Chelsea brought up the lights. "It's like we're mission control," she said. Grade nine, and they were established in the booth, surrounded by old and new tech. An oblong window gave an angel's view of the auditorium. On the stage, the cheerleaders pranced. Patti and Chelsea played the music, a mix with dead spots where the cheerleaders cheered: *From up above to down below we say hello!* Strictly speaking, Patti and Chelsea were up above and looking down, though perhaps the cheerleaders thought differently.

"They got over Rachel's death, I see," said Patti. "They all acted like she was their bestest BFF." Chelsea reached over, tapped the keyboard and brought up Rachel's tribute page. A student had been killed, and now her mysterious killer lurked everywhere, in the town's few alleys, wandering the shore at night, haunting the woods of Hillside Park. National news picked up the small town tale, and someone created the obligatory Facebook tribute page, where people who didn't even *know* Rachel posted sorrowful syrup and pleas for justice and prayers of remembrance. She and Chelsea had known Rachel, a little: Chelsea maybe a little more.

The monitor lit their faces. A new message appeared at the Facebook tribute, a drop of blood: *Spoiled little ho gets killed giving bjs. Suddenly shes a femanazi heroine?*

They stared a moment.

"RIPtroll," said Patti.

"Sick bastard. Oh! What if it's the killer?"

Patti grimaced and they clicked through the name. The account belonged to one *Tony Teerden.* His photo was old black and white, a derelict found wandering Google images.

Brad's voice came over the system. "Music." He stood in front of the stage now. His red-framed specs were visible, even from up above. Chelsea waved. Patti looked over at her friend and raised an eyebrow.

More flips and backflips, cartwheels and turns. *We don't need no music! We don't need no band! All we need is Rose Point, jammin' in the stands! Jammin' in the stands! We're from the Point and we be jammin' in the stands!*

Patti snorted. "*We be jammin'*?"

"They be gangsta, yo."

"Drive-bys around here would be from a tractor." She regretted saying it right away. Chelsea's eyes hid sadness behind purple-tinted lenses.

The cheerleaders continued to bounce about the stage. They performed with the precision and freedom that came with bodies that behaved as the brain directed. The school wanted, after these dark weeks, the return of their small town, a place a killer wasn't still creeping about.

Chelsea stared at the tribute page.

"Let's have some fun with this douchebag." Patti tapped away, created a new account using a sockpuppet e-mail. They found a saucer-eyed manga image for the face. She was now *Terri Teerden*. *Really*, she sent to *Tony*. *All that time alone in your parents' basement, and that's the best you can think of? And "bjs?" Seriously? You ten years old?* A hiccup of a laugh from Chelsea.

The RIPtroller's post unleashed speculation, a new wave of unfounded rumors. Police weren't ruling out anything, and the settings for Rachel's tribute page were changed, so that comments had to be approved. Facebook cancelled *Tony Teerden*'s account, but not before he'd sent *Terri* a reply, an obscenity-filled request that she STFU; if he wanted her opinion, he'd tell her what it should be. Patti smiled and pinged the message. She got the IP and a service provider. *Well*, she thought. Her little worm lived down the shore in Lambton County.

She told Chelsea, but as a pair they took the

matter no further. Chelsea was percolating over her upcoming dinner with Brad's family.

Patti found Brad overly fawning, but Chelsea was even perkier than usual, bouncy-stepped in pink sneakers. She and Brad made a cute couple, until the spring, when they settled back into friendship. Through it all, they remained Tech Club. Only rarely, that first year of high school, did Patti feel truly alone.

* * *

Kirt's chance comes soon. The volunteer who runs St. LARP's website will be retiring to a condo in the Keys. "Now I know you'll probably be angry," says his ma, "but it's not like I committed you to it. I just mentioned that you do IT work. And you seemed to enjoy the variety show."

"You know what, Ma? Maybe I will."

"Oh. Well. You know, dear, it might get you meeting people."

"Don't push it, Ma. I already know enough old ladies."

"We're not *all* old ladies. I'm just saying, keep an open mind."

An open mind, Kirt tells himself, is the one thing he has.

Two years earlier he purchased a pen camera. In the warm seasons he heads up the Lake Huron shore, sits in public places, at tree-shaded benches or dockside patios, pretending to be some old-school poet or compulsive journal-scribbler. He shares the better shots at his site. A good many of his captures are in their early teens, and why not? Girls used to marry at that age.

Now he returns to the same shop with its window-blacked storefront. His new purchase has a removable hard drive and a timer. He pays in cash.

Kimberley comes to mind, for the first time in months. He wishes this tech existed when he knew her. What if he could send it back, through some wormhole, to his fourteen-year-old self? No one would know it existed, so no one could suspect, not her friends, giggling in the changerooms, or Kimberley herself, gymnastically fucking her idiot thug of a boyfriend.

He keeps his appointment, after work Wednesday, with the shiny, enthusiastic young pastor of St. LARP's. They meet under a high-arched ceiling and stained glass, by the flatscreen patched in from a newer tradition. Kirt tells him how much he enjoyed the variety show.

"It *was* good, wasn't it? I wanted to hold it up here, maybe use the new screen a bit. The old ladies overruled me. Washroom and kitchen access. Mostly, though, I think they want the spaces separate. Come on down to my office, Kirt. We'll get a coffee."

The minister shows him the website. Kirt plays all the cards in a stacked deck. He's been IT for years. The company does printing and graphic design so, while, no, he isn't an artist, he can certainly change the visual if the church wants. And, he adds, he hasn't been a church-goer for years, but he's come to realize he's been missing something in his life.

"I see," says the pastor, predatory gleam in his eyes. Sensing he may have invited a discussion, Kirt asks to use the washroom.

Once he's in the basement hall, he closes the door to the men's, and then crosses to the women's. He looks once more at the grate. He twists his screwdriver to the right setting and turns the screws.

Subterranean footsteps echo down the hall. He waits and the sound passes. Each creak and shift of the old place unmans him, and he hates his fear.

He screws the grate back in place.

* * *

sweetiebytes: I don't know what it was like for you. I get lonely at school. My best friend's seeing someone. She makes friends easier than I do. So I don't see her as much.

Magus: What about her new bf?

sweetiebytes: Gf. Bff likes girls. No, not *me*

Magus: Srsly? You hang with a lesbiette? You been holding out on us.

sweetiebytes: Things got bad. You don't wanna hear.

Magus: Try me.

sweetiebytes: What? You're just gonna post what I say for teh lulz.

Magus: WHat? How long we been talking together?

sweetiebytes: Sorry. It's just, her gf's a total girl-jock. Afraid I'm going to out her to her friends, which Im totally not gonna do. Not like that even matters anymore. So her gf basically threatens to kick the crap out of me if I say anything. And my friend does nothing. NOTHING!

Magus: Bitch.

sweetiebytes: Meanest thing on earth is the teenage girl.

Magus: I know they didn't make my life fun.

sweetiebytes: Has there ever been a girl school shooter?

Magus: Your joking now, right?

sweetiebytes: Relax. Listen, life's just shitty right now. Don't worry. Im not gonna go all attention whore and suicide. Become a joke at places like this one. I feel like this is the only place I belong.

Magus: You'll get thru this.

sweetiebytes: Feel sometimes like I'm in some bad American tv show about nerds n jocks.

Magus: Youre not American?

sweetiebytes: Canadian, eh?

Magus: Srsly? Me too.

sweetiebytes: Huron shores.

Magus: STFU!

> **sweetiebytes**: What?

Magus: I'm nearby. WTF, eh?

> **sweetiebytes**: WTF.

Magus: It's fate.

> **sweetiebytes**: Where Huron? Georgian Bay? Gold coast?

Magus: southwest.

> **sweetiebytes**: WTF. We're almost neighbours.

Magus: Fate, sweetiebytes.

*　*　*

The *real* question, Patti asked, was could you call Cassandra's tat a tramp stamp? It rested on her lower back, true, but the ink showed an angel holding a book. Can angels be trampy? Chelsea traced its wings with her fingers as Cassie knelt upright, shirt held up to show the art. Flesh breathed in and out. The two girls had helped Patti onto Cassandra's upsized bed. Patti adjusted her sleep shirt and turned away to examine the bedside shelves, which boasted a collection of books and manga and an assortment of tiny people: Pikachu and Winnie the Pooh, an incomplete set of *Cowboy Bebop* figures, a medieval fool, a tiny china Mother Goose, Mr. Peanut, Miss Scarlet, two Virgin Marys, a dashboard Shriner, and an armed St. Michael, sword up and wings spread. Another angel.

"You totally convinced the tat place you were eighteen?"

"I guess we all have our secrets, right?" Cassie pulled her shirt back down.

"Faye Valentine's so awesome," Chelsea said, following Patti's eyes to the *Bebop* toys on the shelf. "I'd totally be her for Halloween. Except they wouldn't let me in the dance dressed like that. Damn them." Laughter and a mock fist-shake. But there would *be* a Halloween dance this year. With the passing of times things were settling to normal. Grade ten *had* brought a mystery, but not a frightful one. Not a death.

"Faye Valentine?" said Patti. "You'd freeze your ass off waiting in line."

Cassie waited a moment, and then said, "So you really won't tell me?" Chelsea giggled. Cassandra's eyes moved from one girl to the next. "Yarr! Hang the black flag at the end of the mast!"

Chelsea laughed and then said, "Unrelated strange fact. You know the hotel's network reuses, like, the same four passwords?" and they fell over laughing.

The school site had been hacked; parents seeking information got *Lazytown*'s "You are a Pirate" video instead. The hacker's trail wound and twisted and ended at the local hotel's network. People drew conclusions, but neither cops nor school admin could prove a thing. Word spread in whispers. The reputation Patti and Chelsea had been acquiring solidified over the weeks, nods of approval from student rebels, friendly "yar-hars!" Others who had wrinkled their noses at Patti's twisted hobble or worse, effused sympathy like she was some kind of charity case, now saw someone else when she passed: Patti Washington, Hacker Extraordinaire. But she knew she couldn't share details, not anywhere. Shared details came back to haunt you. It was a pity: the *Magus* would be so terribly impressed.

Her communication with the man was born, like so much on the Net, of perverse curiosity.

RIPtrollers turned up in packs. The night after "Tony Teerden" defiled Rachel's Tribute Page, Patti had searched Rachel's name and the details of her death online. She played her keyboard like a music student would a sonata. She found an attempt to rile up interest in Rachel's case, posted in a few places, in identical words. The poster was *the Magus* on his own site, a members-only platform that hosted images and invited commentary. Unwise and shocking pics appeared, bathroom nudes, crime scene photos, stolen kisses and flashes, alongside original material: teens and tweens in their summer clothes, beach girls bending over, hot girls, ugly girls. Another place where basement-dwellers gathered for cheap laughs and fap fodder.

And, she noted, the site had a system for private messages between members, all coded with considerable elegance.

Patti looked again at Chelsea who was staring into Cassandra's eyes, and then she turned away. "If you need me to leave," she said. "I'm used to being *forever alone*."

Chelsea laughed. "That's a lie. You were talking to Steve the other day."

"Steve Obremski?" Cassie looked surprised. "Well, he's *cute*."

"He asked me about the Hack. About which I know nothing, of course."

"Yar-har."

"Fiddle-dee-dee." Chelsea laughed.

"But then we're talking, and he asks about cerebral palsy."

"Ah."

"About all he knows is that I *walk funny* and the plaza near the highway has a donation box. You know, that clothing donation box? In the plaza near the highway?"

"Right."

"So I said 'yeah, Steve, we're after your clothes.' And he goes, 'You wouldn't be the first.'" They laughed. Steve had been conscious he was joking with that scary hacker chick, you know, the disabled girl, the Evil Genius? She felt flattered nonetheless. This was *Steve*: court jester to the jocks. He had a handsome face, symmetrical as one of Cassandra's tiny shelf people.

Of course, he also had a girlfriend, a high-maintenance pleasure model, but not, she supposed, someone a guy like Steve easily left. Still, a girl could dream: a house on a beach with a gas giant and sundry other moons hanging in the sky, and Steve, a Steve who wanted to touch her like Chelsea had touched Cassie's angel tattoo, and if Steve couldn't understand her fantasy's alien sky, she could live with that. She might explain that the gas giant itself would have to be in the star's Goldilocks Zone. He would just nod, she supposed, because if he asked what a Goldilocks Zone was, that could only lead to further questions.

Magus probably understood such things, and she suspected from his posts he craved real-world female contact.

Later, Chelsea assured her nothing occurred. She and Cassie had held hands beneath the covers. Patti shrugged. She had slept nearby, covered in spare flannel blankets, lost in dreams of her own.

*   *   *

Troubles, Kirt explains to his ma, with something like the tone she once used for *lady's problems*. Probably he should just drink less coffee. He can remove the vent in minutes. His hands don't shake so much now.

The congregation uses the upstairs washrooms; the choir takes the ones downstairs. Once the choir has taken its place in the loft, the bowels of St. LARP's rest empty. When he walks those subterranean halls he imagines himself on some old gaming campaign: *You are in a maze of twisty little passages, all alike.* Here be monsters.

He doesn't game anymore, not in the real world. His old friends have moved on, married, settled into work. He wonders if the Slesaks still run a weekly session.

He met Brian Slesak back in ninth grade. At first, they hadn't much liked each other. Kirt had higher hopes, socially, and Slesak, with his acne and loud questions, might as well have been playing the nerd in some teen movie. He played tuba in band; the instrument seemed chosen to enhance an overall comic effect. At first, Kirt laughed with the others, tried to play cool with the girls at school.

Kimberley had teased hair. She sat in front of Kirt in history, and they were paired for a project. She seemed friendly. They talked about themselves as they assembled their material on the Great War, 1914–1918.

"Gymnastics, yeah. Since I was a little girl?"

"So you'd be, you'd be really flexible?"

"Totally. Yeah. There's this like one girl from our school who might make the Olympics. Maybe not the next ones but maybe in 1996?"

"Cool."

"You should see her on the beam. Yeah."

They continued to cut and paste; class computers and Photoshop were still in the future. World War One had a great layout. He saw Kimberley look over at two other girls, who were smirking about something. She flashed her eyes at them, clearly annoyed. Kirt decided she was different from the others, the mewling, preening, make-up-caked creatures that surrounded them.

"Where are they?"

"Uh... Where?"

"The, uh, Olympics? That your friend might be in?"

"Oh! Right, right! Exciting, eh? Uh, *Atlanta.* I mean, I don't think I'll be going, but it's like, this girl might be in, so I could actually go to like, see her. Atlanta's not a far way, right?"

"No. It's in the southern U.S."

"Cool, right? Yeah. The South."

Kirt smiled. "You know, where they say, '*If we get divorced, are we still brother and sister?*'"

She looked at him, cockeyed.

"It was a joke."

"Oh."

He tried to explain.

"We should finish this," she said, and then, "it's looking really good, eh? Yeah."

The Great War, 1914-1918, received 90%. Two days later he passed her in the hall and waved.

"Ooh! There goes that guy you like," another girl said. He felt his stomach tense. A moment later, a second girl giggled.

"Shut up," Kimberley said.

When he returned to his dull blue locker at the end of class, he found someone waiting for him, a square-shaped thug in a Guns 'n' Roses tee. His ears and the lustrous back of his hair stuck out.

"Stay away from Kimberley."

"What? I can talk to who I want to."

The boy moved closer. "She doesn't like you."

"What?" The boy smelled of sweat and smoked meat.

"Would only take one punch."

"I didn't do anything." Kirt looked around and saw Kimberley, standing by. She shook her head. Her face wore a look of either amusement or disgust.

She never spoke to him again after that. He'd see her and this obnoxious jerk walking together in the hall, and Kirt would think about how he was probably taking advantage of that twisty flexibility. He'd try to avoid them, even look away, look down, turn invisible. Her boy slammed him with his elbow once in the hall, sent him into a group of girls. Their jaws opened and shut like angry birds, and they scattered, indignant, and blaming *him*.

At night his mind gave way to dark imaginings. He would break into their homes, ninja-faced, armed, and then rush out across, he supposed, snow-covered shadowy fields. And, of course, he would always get away.

The humiliations lessened with each year. People faded into their lives; the boy who threatened him became a face in the hall. In the eleventh grade, Kimberley's family moved away. By then, he and Slesak had discovered Usenet. They got lost on the cutting edge. They searched for tech news, conspiracy posts, fringe politics, and spent more time than they cared to admit at alt.sex.stories. They also shared anything they thought was funny and any post that contained local news, however mundane.

Workers were digging a rail tunnel from Sarnia to Port Huron, across the river, in the United States. *Boring machine now in Sarnia*, read a headline.

"That explains a *lot*," said Kirt.

Slesak laughed, a braying sort of laugh. "Man, you should post that."

They found more sinister things there, too, from time to time. Slesak grew disturbed easily, but Kirt felt his awareness of the world thickening.

His friend continued to play tuba in band, gamed with the group, dialed into Usenet, worked out a little, and took to tutoring the most unlikely people in math. He started wearing a trilby hat and turned himself into a character, somehow acceptable to people who looked through Kirt, or still smirked when he passed in the hall. In college Brian met tall Augusta, and their place was where the gamers met. They married, moved from an apartment in a half-empty building on Front Street where the wind blew through the walls to a low-rent townhouse and finally, after the first baby came, to a place near Canatara Park. Augusta was polite, but Kirt always felt she looked down on him.

By graduation the cool people seemed to be in computing. Kirt's college classmates did well for themselves. He found steady work and a decent income as IT for a graphics and print shop, but the girls continued to elude him. He never understood. They whined that they were oppressed. *He* certainly was.

He started playing more online, avoided his friends, and mourned the lost, early days of the web. When he created his site he had something like the early Usenet in mind, visually upgraded. His attempts at RIPtrolling had limited appeal, but his creepshots brought crowds of the like-minded.

He retrieves the camera's drive. Maybe he'll have more footage of Mozart Girl—though *that* he might keep for himself. He knows he can't risk too many more attempts here. He will have to find new hunting grounds soon.

The sounds of the choir and the old pipe organ carry from above. He puts the new drive in its place, pockets the old one, screws the vent, and scrabbles down the hallway and back to his ma in the pews.

* * *

sweetiebytes: She looks censored. Like there might have been a bit more showing? Censored, Maggy. Say it ain't so!

Magus: Maybe there's more. Maybe there's not.

sweetiebytes: She looks like a cheerleader.

Magus: Maybe. When she gets to high school.

sweetiebytes: !!!

Magus: I have stuff I don't post.

    sweetiebytes: I bet you do.

Magus: It might be too much for you.

    sweetiebytes: Try me.

Magus: IRL, maybe.

    sweetiebytes: Oh?

Magus: I was thinking about what we said about fate & belonging here.

I know I'm older, but couldn't we just meet?

    sweetiebytes: I'm close to Grand Bend.

Magus: I could do the Bend.

    sweetiebytes: Somewhere public, just in case.

Magus: A public place. I'm good with that.

    sweetiebytes: And meet My Pedophile Lover.

Magus: Hebephile! There's a difference, Jailbyte! But I am an older guy. Thirties.

    sweetiebytes: Hearts can build bridges. Juliet was only thirteen.

Magus: Juliet?

    sweetiebytes: Romeo &.

Magus: Aw.

    sweetiebytes: Yea.

*   *   *

Chelsea's parents are at a movie; her little brother's staying with friends. Patti and Kate sit at the table. Patti helped prepare the pizza, and they've invited her to stay awhile. Chelsea puts her arms around Katie and kisses her.

Patti tries to read the look on Kate's face. Kate, who (Chelsea has confirmed this) posts motivational quotes on her bedroom walls. She now has a place in Chelsea's life to which Patti can never aspire, despite their long history. Patti lives with her mother; her mother's old physics professor sends child support from Toronto. Patti spends time with her mother's parents, but she spent more with Chelsea's family. And now Chelsea has Katie.

Chelsea revels in their differences, the tech girl and the jock. When she discusses their relationship she invokes (unwisely, Patti thinks) *Romeo and Juliet*. She writes a love poem, of sorts. "You'll think it's cheesy," she told Patti, when they were making the pizza.

"The probability's high." She stopped chopping a moment, listened attentively. *Our hearts build a silent bridge* wasn't half bad. "At least you didn't say, *rainbow bridge*."

"Oh, I like that," Chelsea said, sky-eyed.

Patti leaves after dinner, hobbles down the sidewalk, the taste of garlic and pesto and cheese strong beneath the glaze of the strawberries they had for dessert. Her breath freezes under streetlights.

Patti is a patient girl.

*   *   *

sweetiebytes: Not much new this week.

Magus: Almost got a shot of this fat lady like, really fat, gelatinous cube fat. Catching her breath in a stairwell. Couldn't do it without her seeing me. Almost couldn't get down to the rectory cuz she was so fat and slow and blocked the fuggin stairway.

sweetiebytes: Wait, rectory?

Magus: I understand being a lil heavy, but this cow must have someone hold her cheeks apart when she shits.

sweetiebytes: Wait, a CHURCH rectory? YOU go to a CHURCH???

Magus: It's my mother's church! I do volunteer work there.

sweetiebytes: Oh.

sweetiebytes: Wait, you volunteer at a CHURCH?

Magus: Pretty funny, right? I started a couple months ago, helping with their website. Makes ma happy.

sweetiebytes: Awww.

Magus: Also, she cooks once a week.

sweetiebytes: of course she does.

Magus: When I visit her! I have my own place. Anyway,

when can we meet? The public place, Grand Bend?

> **sweetiebytes**: Busy this week. We'll make plans tho. After the recent suckitude in my life, we have to do this.

Magus: Awesome!

> **sweetiebytes**: It's what I need right now.

* * *

The kids in his high school used to hit Grand Bend often. It sits about an hour away, up the shore. He has taken shots there, with his camera pen. He's never seen the place off-season, and hopes the two of them won't be conspicuous.

Kirt packs a bag, things he will need.

His emotions shift, open and then minimize, like windows on the screen. He sees versions of her, Googlepics of hot bespectacled nerdchicks. His mind brims with anticipation at the end to his digital quest, and awards to be clicked and gathered. *It's what I need right now.*

He can give her what she needs.

* * *

The news runs a small photo. His face is elongated, bean-like, with pudginess around the cheeks. He has an unevenly-trimmed moustache and goatee, and brushlike hair. His eyes peer through dirty elliptical spectacles.

Kirt Shane Magden, age 43, arrested in Sarnia,

Ontario. An anonymous tip led to the discovery of a camera in the vent of the women's restroom of a local church, and the subsequent arrest of the suspect.

Patti sucks in her breath.

Kirt Shane Magden. *Magus.*

She took another look at Drop-Drawer Lady. How, Patti asked herself, had she missed the significance of that cultish robe? The woman wore church choir garb; it could not have been more obvious.

Or easy. She amplified Drop-Drawer Lady and her blue robe. Then she image-searched "church" and "choir" with relevant city and county names. Because he had to be in Lambton County, where the ping had led, back in grade nine. She found them in minutes. A quick scope of the choir photo revealed Drop-Drawer Lady beaming proudly among the alto section and, standing with the sopranos, Smiling Crotch Girl.

The church bulletin from November opened to her in a pdf of fonts and clipart and, *With Denny Cooper pursuing his retirement activities away from home, we welcome Kirt Magden, who has volunteered to assist with our website.*

If he was going to make it so easy, he had to expect to get captured.

She experiences a chill, imagining the police entering his private world. She feels regret that she included Chelsea and Kate in the bullshit bully tale she told him, but she figured it made her seem vulnerable, and would draw him closer. She will be especially good to Chelsea, she tells herself, and Kate. And now that their relationship was no longer school speculation, but a matter of simple fact, a couple of girls holding hands in the hallways, a kiss for good luck before games, Patti will stand by if anyone makes too much of it. She smiles. Perhaps she'll post a quote on her bedroom wall:

Do not meddle in the affairs of wizards, for they are subtle and quick to anger.

Three years and, overall, she enjoyed the game. She checks in with the site one last time before it goes black. *Magus* has sent a message to her account:

Listen, I'm in a serious situation right now, no way I cn make the Bend. Send a message to my handle here plus the year you joined the site @gmail

It might be awhile before I can reply. Please wait. I know I can beat this & together we can get over the worlds crap.

To being alone no more

Do You See What I See?

He walked along a rural road, headed in what he hoped was the wrong direction. The sky had that cold winter blue, light without much warmth, and it would be dark soon, like it had that day before. O Holy Night. The first car passed him, but at least it wasn't the Americans, or the cops or... He wasn't thinking clearly, or he wouldn't be standing exposed like that. He had washed up, but his breath, he thought, must be rancid. If he breathed on anyone, they might have to add assault to his rap. His head still pounded but the pills and the syrup were having some effect, and then the wagon pulled over, just ahead. He couldn't remember when he'd last ridden in a station wagon. He wasn't sure anyone made them anymore, but that's what this thing was. He ran to it and looked in the driver's window, which had been rolled down: three old ladies in black winter coats. At least, he thought, they'd be no trouble.

"Might we help?" asked the woman on the passenger side. They had boxes of things in behind, wrapped in clear plastic bags.

He half-assed a story, said his car had gone off the road.

"Oh, well it would be faster to drive back to Zurich," said one woman.

"Where are you going?" he asked.

"The Point, with some stops."

"He could call from Beryl's."

"We're picking up Beryl."

"Beryl lives out in the country."

"That's fine," he said. He could call a tow from anywhere, he explained. He had a roadside service, he insisted, for his imaginary car. Anything, he thought, to put some distance and try to defuckify the situation. He had the money from the night before and a little bit of cough syrup left. If they were going to a point, they had to be heading towards the Bluewater. If he could catch a lift on that, he could slink back to his place in Sarnia and then book.

"I hope you can get them out tonight."

"We do have deliveries to make, before it gets too dark," said the driver, a dark-eyed woman who looked sterner than the rest, like the Old Maid in a kiddie card game.

The woman in the back opened the door and he went in.

"No phone?" he asked. One of the women actually giggled.

"We've been thinking about getting one," said the driver.

"Thank you very much." He looked at the old faces, dark and blue and green eyed, as they introduced themselves: Agnes, Beatrice, and Clare.

"Oh, well thank you for letting us do our good deed for Christmas." The wagon pulled onto the icy rural road. They looked placid enough. He wondered if the news from last night had reached them. He wondered what they were delivering, all those packages behind him.

He never said he was a choirboy and damn it, the world owed him, so why shouldn't he take it? He never got the breaks like other people, never got it all handed to him, so why shouldn't he take it? But he was only a thief and, even after a night of the three of them piling it on, he and the Americans, saying what bad mofos they all were, he wouldn't have called it ending with the three of them being wanted for murder. That was a whole other kind of real. Someone would probably recognize him, too, because he'd been stopping by the Dog Star all year, even if he didn't talk much. Would it matter though? Because maybe Aunt Shirl had been right all along, and maybe something a lot scarier than the cops was after him now.

Of course, if old Shirl were right, *really* right, none of it would matter in a few days. He'd long ago dismissed the old lady as crazy—all old ladies were probably crazy; the women who had given him a lift might be on brake fluid—but he had to wonder now. He was on something himself, of course, the amps the Americans had and a bottle of cough syrup he'd found in the medicine cabinet, because he needed to clear his hangover and juice himself for his escape. He was starting to feel it, the clearing and sparkling in his brain. The one biddy was asking him about the accident and he had to remember his cover; yes, he'd gone off the road and he tried to do the talk about it. He thought they were looking, one to another, using some kind of old lady code. He thought back to the house across from Rainbow Park, and the Dog Star at the other side of downtown, and then the man face down on the pavement.

One man wore a green mask with horns and another foamed and he was dead in a dingy parking lot and God knew what was after them now. After *him.*

And then he saw it, hanging from the dashboard. He'd recognized the candy-cane stripes, thought it was just a Christmas ornament, just like he thought the house across from Rainbow Park had been decked for Christmas, but the ornament turned, spun, and he saw the candy-canes were stuffed in a pouch carried by an old lady, a witch on broomstick, like in a kid's book, but more real.

He took a deep breath.

The old ladies smiled.

They had found him.

*   *   *

It seemed like a good gig, just before meeting the Americans at the Dog Star. He'd done his turn over the years of popping trunks in parking lots and snagging people's Christmas packages, but you couldn't guarantee decent goods and you stood a good chance of getting caught, people just poking out from the shadows of parking garages. And that was back in the big city. In a smaller place it was a particularly bad set-up, though he'd done some pry and grabs in the mall parking lot the week before, some electronics for the Americans and a furry Furby toy for quick turnaround at a local pawn. But if you knew where a good party was happening you could alleycat in, and hide in the dark places. People couldn't hear for shit at a party, half of them would be baked, and if someone saw you, so long as it wasn't the host, you could bluff your way out like, *great party, huh?* If you were really lucky, they'd just blow past you. The key was to grab easy-sell and move quick as a happy ending.

He'd been lying low a year, and his lease would be up in January and then he'd be back in T.O. or at least somewhere more interesting than here, so it was time for a bold move. He had his electronics in his satchel and he knew the Americans would be at the Dog Star, and he'd spotted that party in the two-storey, just a block over, near Rainbow Park. You could see the house from the cracked-pavement parking lot of the old walk-up, the woman, a pretty hot woman, too, and the girls putting drinks on the icy back porch. Worst case scenario, he figured, he could help himself to some free beer. The sun had set by five, and they had only the back porch light on. He had to be most careful here. He cased it from the front first, and saw the cars and the crowd of people with food, doing it all potluck. The house lacked Christmas lights but a bushy wreath hung from the door, and he saw lots of greenery and red berries in the window, just before they slid the curtains closed. They'd probably have some quick saleables and, if luck was with him, a nice pile of coats with stuffed wallets.

He took the long way around to the back again, and made his way into the yard once he saw someone pick up an armful of drink cans. The door was not locked. The kitchen was nearby—bad luck, because that's where everyone ended up at parties— but it was empty, and he could hear the sounds of gathering from another room. The house was dark, candlelit. It was turning out better than he thought. He heard singing, live singing, a child's voice, and moved his way to the stairs.

The kid, a little girl, did "The Holly and the Ivy." He found two bedrooms at the top of the stairs, which he figured for master and, probably, guest. It didn't look like a kid's room, and he saw no coats there. Master it was then, and he stepped inside. The colours were the first thing he noticed, a lot of bright red and black, but no pile of coats, as he'd hoped. They must have had a big closet downstairs. There was a cup like a chalice on the dresser, with the woman's tampons arranged there in plain view.

Then he caught sight of the thing: a winged gargoyle or devil stared back at him, grey stone eyes.

He had no time to ponder home furnishing. He snagged a laptop and a small box of jewelry. He could assess it all later. It was probably best to fence his treasure with the Americans, though he could probably wipe the laptop and pawn it, since he planned to be gone in January.

The singer finished. He looked back at the devil on the dresser and then crept down the stairs.

He heard a crumpling noise, and then realized they were applauding.

He heard a voice, reading or speechifying. They chanted something about watchtowers and outer darkness and directions: East. South. West. North.

He should've just run to the back door, but he saw a shadow in the kitchen and hid in the darkness. He'd never seen a house so dark at a party, all of the candlelight flickering from the living room. He slipped to the front to see if he could get by that way, noticed the blinds even drawn on the front door window, and the door to the room was slightly ajar so he peeked in, just that one, awful moment.

He thought all the red and green was just some kind of elaborate Christmas thing, but then he saw in the uneven tongues of light, the woman with the candles on her head burning and the man in a mask, green and leafy and horned and straight from an old horror movie. Among the small crowd a few people wore robes and one or two didn't look much dressed at all, and candles everywhere and chanting, a knife and a cup and chanting, and what twisted scene had he stumbled into?

The woman breathed fire. He was sure in that glance that she breathed fire.

Just a street over, and across from Rainbow Park. He thought old Shirl had been crazy, all those years ago, with her talks of Satanists and cat sacrifices and the End of Days.

He crept back to the kitchen. The coast was clear, and he headed out the back, quietly, and ran across the darkness of the yard and to the walk-up's parking lot and then booted it, fast enough to cover ground but not running, and finally slowing down halfway to the Dog Star, his breath and lungs freezing and the weight of his goods dragging on his left shoulder.

There had been kids, too, in that room. In Aunt Shirl's stories the Satanic cults always had kids.

Shirl had been counting down, counting down all her life, and it was ten days now and like the song said, *party's over, oops out of time*. It said so in Revelations, said Shirl. He didn't know about that. He never read it. But 2000, she always said: the world would end in the year 2000. He'd recalled Shirl the last New Year's Eve, and laughed, her old warnings and the news about Y2K and nothing happened, the world continued as it had always been. Now it occurred to him she never said *when* in 2000 the world would go. Maybe God was saving it for the last couple days, one last Christmas. He'd seen a devil in a bedroom and a woman breathing fire and a man in a green mask and he thought about Aunt Shirl.

Shirl lasted the longest of Dad's girlfriends and raised them mostly, if anyone did. Crazy old Shirl, who knew how Dad made his extra money and was okay with that, but who talked Bible and reamed them out that time she came home late and he and Cindy were watching that old horror movie. He and his sister stared at a flickering old-time TV, the colours running wrong and a young guy in black by a candle calling out the demon of forbidden knowledge and the arch-devil of the black delights and the cool kids lighting candles and praying to Satan, praying to darkness, and some babe in a robe offering herself in a pentagram. They were going to raise Dracula, who was one of the Princes of Hell. They caught Hell from Shirl; that was for sure. Later, when she caught Cindy and her friends doing Ouija shit, she said the cops had been by. Someone had stabbed a cat, Shirl said, a black cat, and the cops thought it was kids who were into occult. It was bull, of course, Shirl's idea of scaring Cindy straight. He'd had a good laugh, his sister all terrified, fingers picked bloody and jumping when you said boo like she'd seen a snake. Shirl was filled with stories more twisted than that crazy-ass movie, watched every talk show and televangelist who warned of Satanists and even as a kid he thought it was mostly bull, but now he'd seen it for real, the man in the green horned mask and the woman afire. Now maybe, just maybe, they were after him, and Shirl all these years later didn't seem so crazy.

He made it to the Dog Star, the outside crumbling brick and the inside dim lights and yellow. A face lit up and gave him a passing fright, like the people in the house by Rainbow Park had sensed him, had tracked him, but it was a faded plastic Santa Claus the staff had set by the door. Even a place like the Dog Star got into the spirit, with some old Christmas lights mixing with the yellowed ones. He found his Americans at a booth and he knew he couldn't look spooked, but damn, he thought. Just damn.

The lyrics to "The Holly and the Ivy" had been changed. He was sure of it now. He made eye contact with Willy and Spud and then ordered a boilermaker.

Willy and Spud hailed from somewhere near Detroit. Spud had long stringy brown hair and permanently wore an expression between a smile and a scowl. He was a bit heavy. Willy, who always seemed to drive, was tall and slender and clean cut and looked like the class brown-noser, the kid who would turn you in or turn on you when you weren't looking. People ignored you in the Dog Star. They could talk business if they kept their voices low and didn't wave goods around. In Toronto he'd had better fences, and he could move a lot of his own goods, but he'd come under some heat and this town had the border, so the Americans often moved his goods. Willy and Spud could breeze in and out, they said, because the cops ignored good old boys like them in favour of carloads of brothers with their pants hanging down and they asses hanging out.

He looked over at the bar, at the bartender and the bar girls and a couple of guys. The one looked like an old-time biker, with the hair and the beard, but his eyes were softer, kind of girly, even if you could tell he'd seen things, and they'd been things no one wanted to see. Biker hung with the twitchy guy, a skinny fucker with eyes like the crazy preacher Aunt Shirl had eventually fallen for, before she disappeared for good. They were drinking beer and he'd heard they were a bit buggy, the pair of them, people you wanted to steer clear of. He got his drink and joined the Americans in their booth.

The Americans liked the electronics, and knew an old laptop wouldn't rouse any suspicion. Jewellery would cost more, because they couldn't easily explain a jewellery box full of stuff, and anyway, what kind was it? Was it worth the risk? They casually looked at it over the evening, none of it precious and maybe he should consider fencing it himself.

They found the sun and moon pendant, with wry smiling faces like the green man's mask, and the earrings, half-moons and pentacles with amethyst centers. "Jesus, buddy," said Willy. "You knock off the Wicked Witch of the West?" He smiled like the kid who just pulled one over on Mommy and then took a drink of draft.

The thief gave him a look to cover the rapid beat of his heart. "Yeah, well, I ain't all hardcore like you pups."

A few drinks later, they were in the lot, heading for the Americans' battered Ford Escort.

They heard two guys yelling from the food stand in the corner of the lot that appeared to operate year-round.

"What's next for you boys?" He couldn't see them crossing tonight; the border guys would've spotted them as DUI. They had a cheap motel, they said, and they were going to hit Windsor and maybe the Canadian Ballet the next day before crossing back.

"Nothing like the festive season in a strip joint," said Spud, jollily.

Willy opened the driver side door. And a voice from the dark said, "That your car?"

He looked at the guy, two guys, suddenly near them. "Yeah. Not for sale."

The one guy smiled, an older, bug-juiced-looking guy. "Cause you dinged the side of my car."

Willy said that no, he hadn't, his car wasn't even there when they parked, so he needed to get out of their faces. Two against three, the thief thought, but he didn't want any trouble. He hoped the numbers would work to their advantage, but you couldn't tell with buggy guys.

A blink and more shit-talking and then the one

guy was on Willy. He pushed him away and pulled off his belt and started swinging. A buckle caught Willy, who staggered into the open door. He pulled a hunting knife from out of the Escort and Spud grabbed the end of a pop bottle from the ground at the edge of the lot. He tried to say they needed to chill and it might have settled even though Willy was looking angry, a welt on his face, when the twitchy guy, the skinny guy with the mad preacher's eyes from inside the Dog Star just appeared, like he'd been hiding out in the lot, maybe checking cars, and out of the corner of his eye he saw the other guy, the big biker guy with the girly eyes, running towards them and then the twitchy guy grabbed Willy, tried to choke the bastard and Willy twisted around and shanked him with his knife. The twitchy guy stepped forward and fell to the blacktop and there was the big biker guy, heading their way.

"Jesus Christ! Jesus jesus jesus!" And they jumped into the Escort and booted out of the lot. With any luck, no one got a licence, everyone too beer-brained and whiskey-eyed to think, but now they were well and truly shanked and schlonged. The car hit Front Street. Even the plastic Santa looked like it might rat them out.

The Americans headed down the 402 away from the river and the border.

One of them had a friend some miles away, in a rural house. Everyone agreed rural roads were the way to go. He stumbled with a map and tried to remember the way, maybe an hour's drive.

"We're carrying a shit-ton of goods and you fuckin' shank some dickwad in a parking lot!"

"I just turned and it was in." The darkness and snow passed them, outside the window, and kept passing. "Self-defence. Shit, it was self-defence."

They turned off at the next exit.

"And then there's *this* guy."

The thief realized they meant *him*. "I'm no rat." It's the one thing his dad stressed most of all: never rat.

Willy swore. And Spud said, "So what's *your* plan? Hmm? Mr. Prince of Thieves. What's your next move?"

"I was gonna go someplace in January. Hell, you really wanna know, there's an assload of reasons I won't be staying in town, even before this happened. You know me. You know I won't say anything."

"You bet you won't."

Willy popped a few of the amps he had and they headed through falling snow and night glare to an old house somewhere. The thief could not have identified where in his country they were. He kept his eye on Willy's coat and the pocket where he kept his speed.

They had to wake up the owner, a burly, grizzly-faced man who didn't seem overly happy to receive visitors at 3:00 a.m. but understood this was a *situation* and they'd helped him out in the past. Before they even went into the house, a window slid open and a woman's voice from behind the screen asked what the hell was going on?

"Will and Spud. With a guy."

"What the hell." Frost breath came through the screen and the window slid shut again and they ended up crashing in the main room, waking up at times to use the washroom and once to see the woman of the frosty welcome, looking annoyed, head of an older woman on a body and clothes that would've suited her daughter, and the room spinning. He slept uncomfortably, the people in the house near Rainbow Park breathing fire and setting him up for sacrifice, the pentacle earrings moon-magical and calling out like a tracking device. Then he saw the sketchy skinny twitchy guy, down on the pavement in the dark. Blood ran into snow and the plastic Santa smirked and breathed fire.

He woke up and quietly washed away the sweat and stench, as best he could, in a washroom with a window that did too little to block the breeze. He made a quick check of the medicine cabinet: he saw nothing sellable but saw a robo-cough syrup jar, nearly full, and knew a little of that stuff would help clear his head. Next, working with infinite care, he snagged Willy's amps and made his way out. The grizzly guy had stepped out and taken the car. The woman was nowhere he could see.

The snow had stopped. The sun hung low in the blue sky and the air nipped at his face and fingertips. He had no idea which way to go. The year 2001 lurked a week and change away and who knew what great evil things would come crashing into them, because it all seemed possible now. Hadn't they been arguing about that on the TV, that the next century *really* started in 2001? The twitchy guy was dead on the blacktop at the Dog Star and they were wanted men, *really* wanted, the kind of wanted people put up road blocks over, and maybe somewhere the man in the green and horned mask and his women and the creepy children were dancing naked and laughing, just like the Satanists did in Shirl's imagination.

An hour later he was riding a rural road, riding with the ladies in an out-of-date station wagon.

He saw Agnes's eyes in the rear-view, from where the witch was hanging, with her bag of blood-and-white striped candies.

"There's our Mrs. North," said Clare, pointing to a woman who waited at the end of a long rural driveway. "She'll fix you up."

North.

They'd been chanting the directions: east, south, west, and north.

Four old hags.

The car stopped and the back door opened and he saw her, moving towards him, blocking his way. There was a murder of voices as he pushed aside and then he felt something catching him, something he couldn't get away from and he heard calling, cackling, and finally he broke free, he had to break free, because he looked into her eyes and saw fire, and then he ran out into the afternoon where flames exploded around him and figures of darkness surrounded and dragged him into unending silence.

*   *   *

They had to stay, of course, and they used the phone at Beryl's house to contact people waiting on their pies, and St. Michael's Catholic, where Agnes and Clare worshipped and where they were headed next. They baked pies, fruit pies and rhubarb pies and meat pies and shepherd's pies. At first it was a charitable endeavour, especially around the holidays, and that's where a lot of these ones were going. But in recent years, and especially with two of them widowed now and searching for things to do, they were selling them. People loved their pot pies and shepherd's pies in particular, and Agnes's son was guiding them into some kind of full-time business. Here it was, four old women who'd known each other as schoolgirls, in days when they could easily believe in Christmas miracles, could still imagine the angels at work in their lives, four girls who drifted apart with marriage and family, and were now thick as thieves and becoming businesswomen. The Pie Ladies.

Beatrice was most upset by the turn of events. "I was just talking to him," she said.

"Something seemed off," said Agnes, definitively. "Like he'd been drinking. *Drugs.*"

"That would explain the accident," said the cop.

"No idea where he went off the road?"

"We picked him up not ten miles back, but we never did see the car."

"I think he said it was on a sideroad. We were coming from the United Church where Beatrice goes and… Back in Zurich, you know?" The lights of the police cars continued to flash, giving a strange lustre to the snow and warning to drivers passing that way. Cones had been set out roadside and a female officer in a vest stood watch. Beryl's visiting children and the older grandchildren gathered and gawked and offered hot chocolate and coffee. The cops each took a coffee.

"He got caught on my pin," said Beryl North. "And he was screaming and I… I didn't know they'd picked up a man and then I was… Well, I must have been screaming and then…" She took a few deep breaths. "He ran. Like the devil was after him, he ran."

"Such a nice pin, too," said Clare.

The ambulance had come, but the man was beyond medical help. And the women assured the driver of the truck there was nothing he could've done, nothing at all, the man just bolted like that. Terrible timing, so close to Christmas. The driver had been strong, manly, but after talking to the police he sat in the snowbank with his hot chocolate and looked like one of the kids.

The other cop sipped from his coffee. He had been examining their car, and now he was looking at the ornament, hanging from Agnes's rear-view.

"That's *Befana*," she said. "Italian children. Some Portuguese, too, my son says. They sometimes get presents on January 6, from Befana. She's an old friendly witch-woman. You know, the Italian Santa. This one's on a broom, but my son says nowadays she drives an old-fashioned car. So he thought, as a sort of little joke, that I should have one for my old-fashioned station wagon this Christmas." She and the cop had a smile, in spite of the circumstances.

* * *

A couple sat silently in their house across from Rainbow Park. His new mask had been a hit, and her fire was as good as ever, and they'd been happy. The Solstice had gone so well this year, and the potluck afterwards such a success. His vegetarian chili received the highest praise, and the children loved the nachos and her bean dip, and everyone looked forward to another year, to renewal. Who among such a group would have stooped to theft? Who, knowing their acts would return on them, three-fold, would steal from a friend? The world seemed a sadder, darker place.

* * *

Two days before Christmas, the family of skinny, twitchy, wild-eyed Gregory Stumbo, 1973-2000, filed out of a funeral home, with, it seemed, his last friend in the world, the big bearded man with long hair and sad eyes. He was escorted by a tall woman.

Afterwards the pair stood awhile on the sidewalk. "We wish you wouldn't go to that place," she said. "That skeezy bar."

He spoke haltingly. "He had problems, Stumbo, but I never saw him hurt anyone. I never would have thought something like this would happen." He shook his head. "I didn't even get their licence."

"You'll come for Christmas dinner? We've saved a place for you."

"Such good people," he said. They held each other awhile, standing on the sidewalk in the cold.

Acknowledgements

Years of lives, including a few of my own, have shaped this book. That said, *The Con* is a work of fiction. It depicts imaginary people and one extra-terrestrial engaged in activities that probably didn't happen.

I tip my hat to family, friends, fen, long-ago workshop actors, and members of JASNA. I would also like to thank my e-maginary friends, the Noders of e2 and the Bureau-cats of Bureau42, and others who still inhabit ancient online places from a time before social networking sites.

A few, specifically, with reference to this book:

I want to thank Catherine Fitzsimmons of Brain Lag Publishing for her devotion to a project she found "as fascinating as it was bizarre."

I thank my beta readers: Kristen Lee, Tanja Linkes, James McAllister, Darby Shaw, and David E. Smith.

Some beta readers read only a part. Call them gamma readers, but their feedback proved most helpful. Scott Slemmons, Amelia Bornemeier, Natasha Cheeseman, and Katherine Ottaway (among others) provided feedback on the related stories, "Troll Bridge" and "Do You See What I See?" Tanya Jordan checked my math, and Myranda McGaw cast a teenage eye on the younger characters.

Most importantly, I would like to thank Nancy E. G. Quinn, whose singing will be heard in these pages by those who read with care, and without whom this book would not exist.

For those who concern themselves with timelines, the fictitious convention depicted in *The Con* occurs in August of 2015. All other events and historical references line up quite nicely with that. I know of only one anachronism, in Chapter Seven. Most readers won't notice it. Those who do likely won't care. Those who care can be assured that explanations exist that account for the anomaly. It remains in *The Con* as an entertaining puzzle for the curious reader.

Quotations used in the Evensong come from the Anglican Book of Common Prayer.

About the Author

JD DeLuzio grew up in northern Ontario and now lives midway between Detroit and Toronto with his wife, Nancy. He has written several short stories, numerous reviews (many at Bureau42.com), several articles, and one collection of short fiction, *Snow-Man's Land*. As an educator, he has workshopped a number of original theatrical productions with youth. He also frequently runs panels at SF, pop culture, and literary events.